Amber in the Moment, or God Bless You, Mr. Vonnegut!

Kirk Vonnegut

Published by
Keith Massie Self-Publishing

Nothing in this book is true.
(except the previous sentence)

ISBN-13: 978-1500177638
Printed by createspace.com.

June 2014

Dedicated to Owen Elmore, Bernard Gallagher, and Arthur Rankin, who were prisoners with me in the Slaughterhouse Five of Alexandria, LA

"Imitation is the best form of flattery."
–Charles Caleb Colton

ONE

Vonnegut, Slaughter House Five, Tralfamadorians'
response to Billy Pilgrim.

...

This book is written by Kurt Vonnegut. That sentence is
true but should have an asterisk after it.

The asterisk is a reference mark to highlight an
omission or doubtful content. It's also used for
decoration sometimes.

Since Kurt has been dead for seven years now, you may see why the asterisk is needed for the first sentence. An idiot may think that the first sentence is a lie, but omission of information and active deception are two, very different things. The omission is central to the story he is writing now and you are reading.

...

Walt Disney was cryogenically-frozen to be thawed out at a future time and cured of the disease that killed him. That sentence is a lie. It doesn't need an asterisk. It is, however, a common urban myth. Myth is just a fancy word for lie. It is believed that freezing the human body slows down the cellular process and bright people in the future would have the know-how to unfreeze a frozen person. If they have that knowledge, they surely can fix whatever was originally broken in the cryogenically-frozen person. At least, that's what the myth would have us think. Like you, I hate being lied to.

...

Listen:

During the last month of Vonnegut's life, he took part in an experiment not so different from the urban myth of Disney's cryogenic animation. It seems ironic that an animator would want to stop animating, but that's exactly what the lie would lead us to believe. The experiment was called the Thought Transfer project and was symbolized by two T's placed so close to each other that they touched. It looked like this:

The TT project froze numerous thoughts of the participant and stored them. Millions of thoughts were frozen, stored in the amber of the moment. They were contained in thought bubbles much like those found in newspaper cartoons. They looked like this:

> Off to my book club while my new machine does my Whites, Goodbye,

> Bess get movin'...deys' done did get themselves a new machine! We ain't needed 'no mo'

Unlike the cartoon bubbles that any literate child could read, the thought bubbles of the TT project were coded in a cryptography that even the brilliant scientists running the project could not decipher. How they ever believed that there was information in those bubbles is beyond me. Being good packrats though, the scientist stored the bubbles and hoped someone smarter than them would figure out what the hell they meant.

...

Fifteen hundred individuals were selected to participate in the TT project. Vonnegut got on the list by pulling a few strings. Most participants were just average Joes and Janes. Two of those Joes and Janes were Alice Winner and Ted Johnston. Alice was a kindergartner teacher at Elmwood elementary and an amateur photographer. Two days before she was to be herded off to the secret location of the TT project, she met her end. As an urban dweller, Alice photographed urban settings. People can only picture what they can see. At the unset of her summer vacation, she decided to expand her hobby in a new direction. She set off to the woods to take nature pictures. Anyone who saw her would know immediately that she was an urban dweller. She wore a black skirt, red blouse, and high heels as she walked into the forest. Seeing a beaver, she got ready to take her first nature picture. Excited, she moved closer to get a better shot. Her high heel snapped and startled the beaver. It rushed her. Attempting to run from it, she fell down because the heel of her nice, new shoe had broken. The beaver pounced and gnawed her right leg. She was a fighter, though. Bending at the waist, she readied her arm to strike back at the monster. It saw an opening and chopped hard at her neck severing her carotid artery. The carotid artery is one of the largest arteries in the human body. The largest is the femoral. Alice bled to death quite quickly. Dying, she felt sad that she would never get a picture of the cute creature. Had she taken one, it would have looked like this:

Her thoughts were lost to that pesky thing known as death. So it goes.

Ted was a professor at Peanut University. On the last day of his life, he was wearing a jacket expressing where he worked. It looked like this:

Ted was passionate about his university. A group in his city that called themselves the Pluto gang were not so enthused by the university. Unlike Ted's jacket, they wore one that looked like this:

Members of the gang would often berate those associated with the school by saying "PU, you stink." PU was the initials of the school, but it was also a sound people would say when they smelled something atrocious. Walking home from school four days before he was to attend the TT project, Ted passed a young man who said, "PU, you stink." It was the first time Ted heard the expression, and he was infuriated by it. Not knowing the connection of the expression to a gang, Ted changed course as to lecture the young man. According to his teaching evaluations, Professor Johnston was a good lecturer.

"What the hell did you say?" Ted said authoritatively.

"You heard me," the young man replied.

"Well…" was the last words out of Ted's mouth before the 4 other gang members lurking in the shadows stabbed him to death. Ted's brilliant ideas would never make it to the TT project because of his not-so-brilliant thoughts on that evening. So it goes.

…

Poor Alice and Ted were not the only ones to pass away before having the chance to transfer their thoughts. Six fraternity brothers from Pi Pi Pi, whose moniker was "Try Pie" and was a misogynistic and heteronormative proclamation, died two weeks before the project. They had gone on a trip to see the Grand Canyon, a large hole on the planet Earth. Deciding to be adventurous and take a different route back to their school in Nevada, they got lost in Zion National Park at night. The road curved dangerously near cliffs and had no guardrails. Their thoughts got left at the bottom of a canyon when their rented SUV blew a tire and went off the road. One of the Try Pie's thought the SUV should have had a sign on it warning them of the risks of using it. His imagined sign looked like this:

THIS CAR

IS A LEMON!

Miraculously, he survived the initial impact of the SUV with the floor of the ravine. Just before the blow out, he had taken his shoes off and was airing out his bare feet by placing them out the window. The impact of the crash had shattered both his tibias and fibulas, cracked one of his femurs, broke two of his ribs, and cut a small laceration under his right eye. The adrenaline rush he felt gave him the courage to crawl out of the mangled SUV. He took five steps from the crash site and became dinner for two hungry and courageous coyotes who had went to investigate the crazy sound they heard. Investigators would find what remained of him next to these:

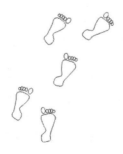

...

They had rented the SUV from Enterprise rather than Hertz. Briefly, they had discussed changing their company choice when they went to pick up the SUV at the airport and saw a Hertz shuttle. It looked like this:

The fraternity president had said, "No, we better not because it hurts." They laughed stupidly like only fraternity brothers can. Each took turns playing on the word Hertz with hurts. Nobody was laughing now that they were down at the bottom of a canyon. So it goes. The Hertz SUV that they didn't rent would not have blown a tire. It would have been carjacked when they got in it to leave their hotel near the Grand Canyon. Thus, of the fifteen hundred participants located to take part in the TT project, only fourteen hundred and ninety-two would actively take part. That number looks like this when written numerically:

1492

...

Vonnegut was met by two representatives of the TT project at his Manhattan home on the evening before the thought extraction was to occur. They informed him that he was not to know the location of the TT project as it was classified by the US government. They liked to keep a lot of secrets. Vonnegut prepared his things. The two gentlemen escorted him to his driveway where he saw a black, 2007 Chrysler Voyager. It was a van with no labels indicating that it was part of the TT project's fleet. One way to keep things secret was to not label your transportation. As the older of the two gentlemen rounded the front to go to the driver's door, the young TT agent opened the side door for Vonnegut. Vonnegut saw three individuals already in the van. None of them were Alice, Ted, or part of the Tri-Pie fraternity. Each of them had died recently, so they couldn't make it. The three individuals in the van varied in stature but each shared a common trait. They had bags over their heads.

Vonnegut turned to see the agent ready a bag for his head. Having bagged Vonnegut, the two agents started off on their trip to a secret location paid for by taxpayer's dollar yet unknown to all. As the van made its first turn out of Vonnegut's neighborhood, the closest bagged individual to Vonnegut said, "PU, you stink." He was Joe Lazzaro, a distant relative of Paul Lazzaro who had fought in the Second World War. Joe had been one of the gang members responsible for Professor Ted Johnston's untimely end. His statement was not one related to Peanut University because he couldn't see anything from his bagged head. No one can see anything when you placed a bag over their head. It was a statement acknowledging that Vonnegut had been working so diligently over the last couple days as to prepare for the coming TT project that he had forgotten to shower. Such acknowledgement is not what most people want.

TWO

Listen:

I sat down at my kitchen table and had breakfast. Two eggs, a piece of rye toast, and four bacon strips stared back at me. A glass of apple juice accompanied the meal. It came from apples that look like this:

I only ate it because it was known as the Breakfast of Champions. I wasn't a champion, but I wanted to be. I was a Customer Service Representative or CSR. Businesses seemed to use acronyms for everything. Then again, so did young people when they sent texts. One of the few benefits of my job was that it had flexible hours or FHs, which was nice.

I opened a book by Klondyke Bass, my new, favorite author. Bass was a science fiction writer. Mr. Rozevater, my superior, had introduced me to the strange world of Bass. God Bless You, Mr. Rozevater for telling me about Bass. Rozevater claimed to be Bass's number one fan and had written him correspondence on several occasions. Bass never replied to any of the letters.

...

Bass had written a number of books and short stories. I was reading Bass's tale entitled, *Gorge and*

Go Green, which centered on a future solution to climate change, the "chow cow." Scientists had found that the methane gas released by cows, in the form of farts and excrement, contributed to global warming. A normal cow looked like this:

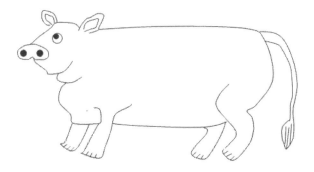

They worked adamantly to create a cow that had two heads, one on each end of its body and no tail. A smaller digestive tract was engineered, and the cow defecated through a small opening on its underbelly. This new and improved beast ate twice as much but retained seven times as much of its food. Unexpectedly, it not only decreased the methane in the atmosphere but also decreased world hunger. Bass thought himself clever that the *Gorge* in his title referred to both the cow's intake and its use as a food source. He also patted himself on the back for making the genetic alteration have the odd side effect of making the cow's skin green. Green is used to denote environmentally friendly acts. The crafty scientists called it the "chow cow" because you didn't know if it was coming or going. While the geneticists were brilliant at making such a divine creation, they were no wordsmiths and named it "chow" rather than "ciao" cow. The "chow" stuck because other idiots thought it was a reference to the cow's food intake. Bass's story was a tragedy. The chow cow had saved the planet from getting too hot but had nearly made Homo sapiens extinct. Life expectancy dropped radically as human obesity skyrocketed due to the vast amount of food. Many died from a rare disease contracted from eating the genetically engineered meat. Explosive diarrhea from the disease caused people to suddenly excrete all the water from their body out their ass; they died, where they stood, in minutes from the dehydration. When bystanders saw the event take place in the street, they would say "ciao" to the stranger.

...

I finished my food and headed to work. Walking home after a full day of work, I saw a truck on the road and had to chuckle. It looked like this:

A peer is someone similar to you. To be peerless is to be without someone like you. It was obvious that the trailers were similar, yet the company has selected to label them as if they were not. Labels are silly sometimes. The sight of the silly truck reminded me of a book by Sherry Turkle about how Americans think about technology. Its title said it all, Alone Together: Why We Expect More from Technology and Less from Each Other. These peerless trailers were alone together, barely linked, yet right next to each other.

When I reached my apartment, an event would happen that would change the course of my life. Mother Night was approaching, and with her, a dramatic shift in my life. I was not ready for it, but it would happen nonetheless. The amber of the moment would take over, and there was nothing I could do to stop it.

Readying myself for bed, the first thought bubble penetrated my psyche. I shook violently and threw up my dinner. I had had chicken from a fast food restaurant. It had looked like this:

It didn't look like that now. The shakes became more violent. I cried out, "Why me?" Then, an image appeared in my mind. It said: Vonnegut, Slaughter House Five, Tralfamadorians' response to Billy Pilgrim. As the message repeated itself, the shakes became more powerful. I ached and wanted it to stop. Trying to compose myself, I grabbed a pen from the desk and wrote the words down. The tremors subsided slightly. Writing the thoughts down seemed to help. I deduced that I should write them again. I took out my laptop and typed them. The agony dispersed. The pain was over. For now.

THREE

The Voyager made three more stops over the next six hours. At the first stop, the TT agents didn't load a new participant into the van. They had arrived at Professor Johnston's house only to find that he had been murdered. They had seven people on their list to acquire, but they would only bring six to their superiors. Seven people minus one dead person equals six persons. Both hoped they would not get in trouble for not bringing Johnston. It was a dumb thing to think since they had no control over his demise.

At the next two stops, others were loaded into the van. The perfume of the last one suffocated those already present. It was heavy and putrid. Merriam Beauveax was a middle-aged, French immigrant who had readied herself for the project's arrival by dressing as if to go to a nightclub. She wore high heels similar to those Alice Winner was wearing when she was killed. Fishnet stockings, a short skirt, a sheer blouse, and enough makeup to have kept zombie movies in business for two years rounded out her attire. Her best friends, Judy Thompson and Hilda Hurley, had given her a bottle of expensive perfume for her last birthday. Wanting to make a good impression, she had showered herself in it. As the younger TT agent started to place the bag over her, she said, "N'abîmer pas mon maquillage." It was too late. The bag was over her head and her mascara on her cheeks. And so on.

···

Lazzaro, Vonnegut, and two of the other participants coughed violently. The perfume burned their covered eyes and irritated their breathing, which was tough enough with a bag over your head. The only person unaffected was Tyler Jackson. He had been a sanitation worker and had lost his sense of smell years ago.

"PU, you stink," Lazzaro said.

"Can we do something about that stench?," another asked of the TT agents.

In the front of the van, the TT agents were already contemplating how to deal with the issue without losing too much time. There was a schedule to keep and consequences if they didn't get the participants to the right place at the right time.

The van made a sharp left and stopped suddenly. Vonnegut heard the two front doors open and close. There was an echo as the van's side door slid open.

"124R," the young TT agent said.

He was referencing Merriam. All participants no longer had a name while in the experiment. They were given a code. Vonnegut was 124C.

•••

In his Manhattan home, Vonnegut had chuckled when they told him his name was 124C. It was the number assigned to Ralph, the robot of science fiction writer Hugo Gernsback. Vonnegut had read some of Gernsback's science fiction. Gernsback was considered the Father of Science Fiction, as if a genre was created through sexual reproduction. When the agents told him his number, Vonnegut had a light switch of awareness turn on. A light switch looks like this:

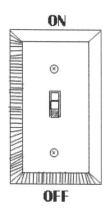

He thought it clever that Gernsback's tale of
Ralph124C about the future had phonetically
incorporated "One to foresee." Oddly, 224C was the
only Siamese or conjoined twin to participate in the TT
Project.

...

"124R," the older TT agent repeated.
Merriam was so distraught by the thought that her
makeup was ruined that she had temporarily forgotten
her assigned code.
        "Oui, I mean, yes," she mumbled through the
bag.
The two agents took her hands and helped her out of the
van as to not have her bump her head.
Her high heels clacked against cold concrete.
Clink, clink, clink, clink.
Vonnegut heard what sounded like quarters being
deposited into a machine.

...

Brody O'Malley was excited for the upcoming weekend party. His fraternity, the Tri-Pies at Peanut University, had a yearly end-of-the-Spring-term party. The party was one of the biggest of the year at PU. You stink, he thought to himself taking a whiff of his underarm as he threw his backpack over his shoulders. The backpack contained the items he had just bought at the store. They included twelve packs of C batteries, Sudafed, and Drano. Brody was a Chemistry major and planned to cook up a new and improved version of methamphetamine. The drug had Drano in it. The product's label looked like this:

DRĀNO

If taken alone, Drano could kill someone. There were even reports of people committing suicide by doing so. Mary Hepburn, a friend of Brody's parents, had contemplated suicide. She had considered placing a garment bag over her head or drinking Drano, but she settled for dying from a shark attack thirty-one years later. So it goes.

With his backpack firmly in place, Brody hopped on his skateboard and headed back to campus. Halfway down the street, a black van almost hit him as it turned sharply to enter the local car wash. Brody had to ride into the grassy patch near the sidewalk to keep from slamming into the maniac van. The sudden change of speed had thrown him from the board. He was used to it. He landed on his feet and began running to maintain his balance. Slowing his pace, he finally came to a stop. His skateboard was about twenty yards away. He began to walk back to it.

As he got about a third of the way back to where his skate board sat in the grass, he heard the van door open. For some reason, it piqued his curiosity, so he stopped momentarily to see what the maniacs that almost hit him were doing. Two men had taken another, who had a bag over their head, out of the van.

The bright lights of the nearby strip club illuminated Brody's view of the van and its occupants. The club was called Fairy Land and had a Player Piano rather than a DJ for stripper's to dance to. It had a sign that looked like this:

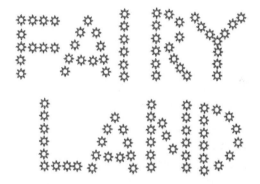

Under the bright lights was a marquee. Its four words help clarify that it was a fully nude strip club. The words were:

WIDE-OPEN

BEAVERS

INSIDE /

Brody used the lights of Fairly Land to watch the events unfolding in the car wash stall. Two men had taken a third man out of the van. The third person was being degraded. He wore women's clothes and had a bag over his head. Brody assumed this was a hazing ritual. Like all good humans, Brody linked what he didn't understand to that which he did. He watched anticipating the events to come.

...

The thing was:

The two TT agents had to get the stink off Merriam. They didn't want to violate protocol. Protocol said that once the bag was in place, it could not be removed until the final destination. As agents of a government program, they didn't think. They simply followed protocol like mindless machines. Rinsing someone with high pressure water didn't violate the protocol though. It was an odd protocol.

Being clever, they went to the car wash and sprayed her down with the high pressure water. Although she was standing in a car wash stall rather than sitting in an interrogation room, Merriam experienced a version of waterboarding. Waterboarding violated International law, but US government agencies didn't seem to care. At least, the two TT agents didn't.

Rather than think that she was being cleaned of the retched smell of her perfume, Merriam thought she was being interrogated.

Between blasts of high pressure water to the face, she exclaimed, "Okay, okay, I told Judy

Thompson what I had been chosen for, but I didn't tell Hilda."

"I swear, I didn't tell Hilda," she continued. It was a lie. She had told Hilda, but she liked Hilda more than Judy. Sometimes, people are good at lying. Like you, I hate being lied to.
The two TT agents looked at each other. They knew they had to report this to their superiors.

...

Brody watched with juvenile excitement at the torture of poor Merriam. He was one of the dipshits in the US who thought hurting people was cool. As he watched, he thought:

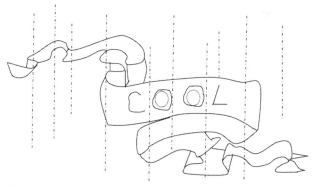

As the two men placed the defeated and wet person with the bag on their head back into the van, Brody ran over to his skateboard. He wanted to get back to his frat house and tell his fraternity brothers all about his new idea for hazing pledges.

Riding his skateboard quickly, he passed the home of J.A. Hoobler. It had a pink flamingo on the front lawn. A flamingo looked like this:

He knew it was Mr. Hoobler's house because the mailbox had his name on it. It looked like this:

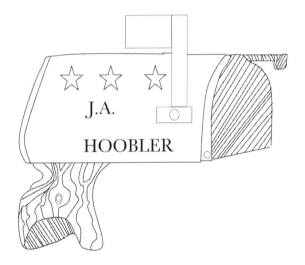

Being a young idiot, Brody thought the flag on the mailbox should be down. He had never sent a letter, only email. Passing the mailbox, he reached over and pushed the flag down.

FOUR

Listen:

After a full day of traveling by van, train, and plane, the TT participants reached their final destination. I can't tell you where it was. Even if I did know, I wouldn't tell you because the location is classified.

All the TT participants still had bags over their heads as they were herded to the main TT facility. They passed the facility's numerous layers of defense against intrusion. The first looked like this:

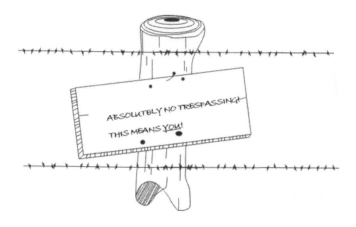

None of them saw the sign because of the bag, but the world doesn't end just because you close your eyes. The sign existed because the TT agents saw it.

...

Dr. Darnell Durling Heath was the individual in charge of the facility. He went by Durling. On his desk, was a name plate to make that clear. It looked like this:

DURLING HEATH

    As he sat at his desk with the nameplate on it, one of his subordinates came in to tell him that all the participants had reached the facility. At least the ones who were still alive. Heath closed the book he was reading on Bokononism and set it on top of his Ghost Shirt Society newsletter. He walked over to the white board on his office wall. It had a multitude of scientific equations on it. Some were chemistry and looked like this:

Others were related to quantum physics. One of those had Einstein's famous equation imbedded in it. It looked like this:

$$E = Mc^2$$

The equation also had the infinity sign in multiple places. The infinity sign looks like the number eight had gotten drunk one night and fallen over. It looked like this:

Heath hoped that the experiment of thought transfer would go without a hitch. Years had gone into its development. Scientists had theorized how to store linguistically-constructed thought, so no animal testing could take place. Animals don't have linguistically-constructed thoughts. The Guinea pigs were human. Though PETA didn't know about the classified project, they would have been happy that no animals were at risk of harm, only humans.

...

While some of the major ideas for the possibility of thought transfer were achieved in experimental neuropsychology and neurophysiology, the scientists made a major breakthrough after watching a popular movie. Jurassic Park was a movie about dinosaurs being brought back from extinction. The process for reanimating the beasts had a few steps. First, get a mosquito that had sucked blood from a dinosaur and, then, got trapped in the sap of a tree. Second, take a special syringe and extract the dino-blood. The syringe looked like this:

Third, take the dino-DNA and blend it with that of a bird, like a chicken. A chicken looks like this:

Last, wait for the eggs of the creation to hatch and grow up to be a real dinosaur like a stegosaurus. A stegosaurus looks like this:

Like the blood in the mosquito trapped in the sap, scientist began thinking of individuals' thoughts as trapped in the amber of the moment. They need only find the process to extract those thoughts from the dense amber. Through tireless work, they had potentially found that process. After extracting the thoughts, the scientists had little time to store them. The half-life for a thought was miniscule. The thought was frozen through a process using a recently discovered molecule. It was called Ice-Nine, and it looked like this under a special microscope:

The participants were there to find out if the scientists' procedure would work.

...

Each participant had been herded into the facility and given their own, individual room. The rooms were small, institutional, and musty. The bags were removed from their sweaty heads only after they were placed in their assigned room. The room had a cot, pillow, blanket, toilet, sink, mirror or leak, and a single window. It was not too different from some prison cells. Vonnegut settled into the cot that they had provided for him. It reminded him of his days in the military. The cot was olive green, but its unyielding nature was what reminded him of the past the most. He lay on the cot and thought about what to think when his time would come to have his thoughts transferred. Being an author, it had to be a good story. The story, this story, would be his last novel and replace Timequake as his finale. He would end his tales by getting them out of the 90s. The story should start with the Tralfamadorians' response to Billy Pilgrim and I should let the reader know it comes from my book, he thought.

···

But to continue:

Dr. Heath wanted to locate his celebrity participant and ask why he had pulled strings to get listed among the participants. If Heath had ever gotten his answer, he would have known that Vonnegut did not expect to live much longer and wanted to get one more novel out. Vonnegut believed he could think the novel into existence faster than he could type it up.

Heath left his office and headed down the long hallway. He passed a door that looked like this:

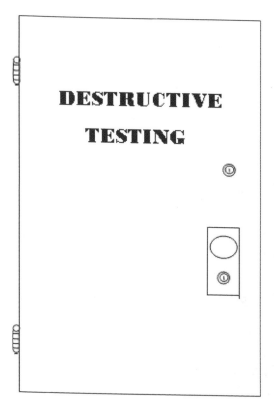

DESTRUCTIVE
TESTING

His footsteps echoed in the long hall. He exited the main building and walked across the facility's grounds to one of the many temporary buildings used to house the participants. Moments later a knock came on Vonnegut's door.

"Are you decent?" a voice asked.

•••

As Heath was walking to see his celebrity participant, an event unfolded on the grounds that would need to be covered up. Conspiracy nutcases thought the government did a lot of covering up. They thought the government had something to do with the JFK assassination, 9/11, the Sandy Hook shooting, and the Boston Marathon bombing. President Nixon would have liked a world like that. Fact was the government is fairly inept at covering up big things. Lucky for Heath, this was a smaller thing.

After arriving at her assigned room, Merriam Beauveax was more than emotionally rattled. She was on the precipice of a nervous breakdown and stared into the abyss as she saw herself in the small mirror in her room. Her makeup, which she had taken so much time to put on, was everywhere. Like her mascara, rouge, and eye liner, her thoughts were going every which way. The waterboarding that she had experienced yesterday had permanently disrupted her brain. The brain is sometimes considered the nerve center, and Merriam's looked like this now:

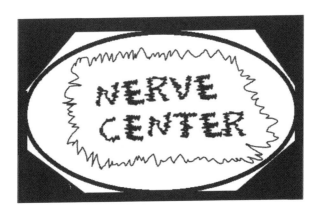

The one item in the room that was not like a prison cell was the mirror, and Merriam knew why. She had dated an ex-con years ago when she had first arrived in the country and had had to work as a stripper.

She had worked at a place called Fairy Land. Its sign looked like this:

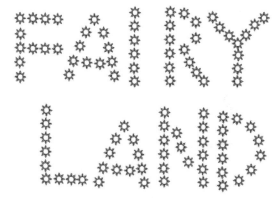

The previous boyfriend and felon had told her that mirrors were weapons. At first, she had thought his claim was that they could cause harm to you if you didn't put make up on and look your best in them. The felon was not talking about such psychological pain. He was talking about physical harm. She came to understand that if the mirror were broken, which incidentally was suppose to bring seven years bad luck, you could use the shards like a knife.

She thought about what to do with the shards. Briefly, she considered suicide. Her nerve center's wiring was messed up, but it was not that defunct. Then, she pondered on the possibility of calling the guard outside and stabbing him. It would never work, she thought. She was not aggressive by nature. What if, she thought, I attempted suicide. They would come and save her and release her from her obligation to take part in the experiment. She would be psychologically unfit to be a part of it. It was a good plan except the bowels of her guard did not seem to know about it.

Pulling the sleeve of her blouse down over her hand, she punched the mirror. It broke into shards, and the clock of seven years bad luck started counting down. Taking a sharp, silver sliver, she raked it across the side of her neck. She wanted it to appear real, so she had pushed hard. Unfortunately, it was too hard. She had caught her carotid artery and opened it slightly. If Alice Winner were still around, she could have told Merriam to be careful. Merriam screamed in pain and horror as the blood shot from the wound.

"Help!, help!," she shouted. They would come soon, she thought.

Unfortunately, the only guard assigned to her corridor was taking a dump. He was in no hurry to finish and was reading the newest issue of Sports Illustrated. The article was about football. A football looks like this:

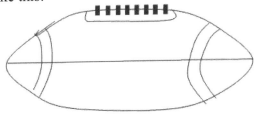

Merriam could feel her consciousness waning. Oh, my, she thought, Judy and Hilda will believe that I killed myself. Judy and Hilda would hear about her death from another TT participant that they knew. Karen Von Gleiss was one of the few participants who not only had a successful thought transfer but also the only remaining participant who knew Judy and Hilda. It was still a very juvenile process with numerous glitches.

Merriam rushed to write a non-suicide note stating that it was an accident. There were no pens and no paper. The only liquid was her blood, and there was plenty of it. Frantically, she dipped her finger in the warm blood and wrote "Accident" on the floor. As she finished the "t" of the word, she lost consciousness. Her body fell near the blood-written word. The few pints left in her were more than enough to spill out and cover her message. Her seven years of bad luck expired, and so did she. So it goes.

...

Vonnegut heard a knock on his door and moments later a question.

"Yeah, I'm decent," he stated.

A short, portly man in his late fifties entered. It was Dr. Darnell Durling Heath. Vonnegut was slightly annoyed by the disruption to his thoughts. He had this book to think up and only one night to complete it.

After formally introducing himself to Vonnegut, the head of the program sat on the cot.

"Do you know that your name is quite similar to a character in one of my books?" Vonnegut asked.

"No, I didn't."

Heath had not read a single work of Vonnegut's. He was only visiting him as to tell his friends that he had met the famous author.

Their awkward conversation was friendly and cordial. Both men could feel the power dynamic. Heath was trying to place Vonnegut in a subordinate role, and Vonnegut knew it. On an average day, Vonnegut would simply assume the role and not make waves. This was not an average day. It was the last hours available to him in order to think through his last novel. He was annoyed by Heath's bantering and banality.

Given Heath's arrogance and Vonnegut's quick wit, the conversation devolved rapidly. At one point, the following dialog took place:

"People who think they know everything are annoyance to those of us who do," said Heath.

"Do you know who originally said that?" asked Vonnegut.

"No, I just thought it up."

"Oh," said Vonnegut grinning devilishly. Vonnegut knew that it was first said by Isaac Asimov. It clearly showed that Heath didn't know everything. Heath was smart enough to realize Vonnegut's undermining.

Later, they shared more verbal barbs. Heath attacked the academic reputation of Vonnegut's brother, Bernard. Bernard was a well-known physicist and expert on thunderstorms. He had already passed away. So it goes.

Vonnegut came to his brother's defense, and Heath felt hurt by his words.

The program director came back with, "If you were my brother, I'd poison your soda."

Echoing Winston Churchill, Vonnegut snapped back, "If you were my brother, I'd drink it."

Vonnegut had had enough of Heath and was infuriated that the comment about drinking poisoned soda brought back memories of his failed suicide attempt and his mother's successful one. He went into a torrent of comments degrading Heath.

"Mr. Expert, do you know that the word 'expert' comes from the root 'pert' meaning effective and the prefix 'ex' which means not? Your wife told me that as she referenced your inability to please her."

And "Everyone is entitled to be stupid, but you, sir, are abusing the privilege."

The rant continued, and, dejected, Heath left the room in the middle of it with his head down. As he exited, he shouted back, "Stop bloody hounding me!"

As the door closed, Vonnegut smiled. He could get back to his thinking and this novel.

•••

It is important to make clear that Vonnegut was not usually so mean to people. He was an easygoing spirit. He didn't mind making fun of characters in his novels. But those were fictitious characters, and Heath was real. Vonnegut was only mean because he had so much work to get done. Writing a novel took time, and time was something he was running out of. He had written Sirens of the Titans quickly, but he knew he was a young man then and full of ideas. Now, he was older and his thinking slower and more calculated.

•••

Everyone associated with the TT project had the same misconception regarding it. The scientists had believed that a future technology would directly unlock the encrypted words of the thoughts. The TT scientist had hoped that they could develop the technology to read the thoughts, but they couldn't. Storing the thoughts, the Project scientists assumed someone in the future would have the necessary technology. The future didn't have the technology, but they did have an indirect way to get at the bubbles.

Conversations at the facility noted that the two T's in the project's name could symbolize two individuals. One was the "original" thinker, and the other was the "transferred-to" thinker. Unknown to them, a third T was needed to complete the process. The Transistor was a person who could decode the thought bubbles of the "original" and get it to the "transferred-to" thinker. I was Vonnegut's Transistor.

The technical process is impossible for me to explain since I don't have a college degree. All I understand is that Vonnegut's bubbles were obtained before his death. They were stored. In the future, a person I call the Faxer has the technology to send the bubbles to my psyche causing tremendous discomfort until they are typed. I call the person the Faxer because it is like he is faxing the thoughts into my mind. I cannot escape them. I am caught in the amber of the moment. Thus, the ideas from the past head to the future to be sent to the present. In the present, they are written. The written materials make their way through time, like everything else, and arrive on the book shelf of the Faxer and his friends. It was an indirect route, but it worked.

...

This says it is written by Kirk Vonnegut. That is a pseudonym though. Pseudonyms are fake names people use when they write something. They are lies. Like you, I hate being lied to.

My name is actually Keith Massie. I'm only using the pseudonym so the Faxer can have Kurt Vonnegut's work, this work, catalogued with his other writings in the future library. The Faxer will probably appreciate that. Vonnegut thought it would be transferred to someone directly in the future, so he expected to be the author. They *are* his words.

•••

Listen:

More than a millennium in the future, the Faxer walked into the lab of the Bluebird Farm facility, which was designed to unleash the hidden thoughts buried in the thought bubbles of the past. The Bluebird Farm had a sign outside that looked like this:

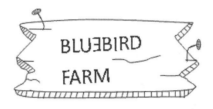

Everyone working for the facility knew that the Blu represented the past, Bird was the codename for the present, and the backward E symbolized the Transistor who would link the past to the present. The Faxer prepared to send the first stored thought bubble into the past. The Faxer opened the draw marked "Lazzaro 1," and took a single item out. It was a thought bubble wrapped with a band stating it must remain sanitary. The band looked like this:

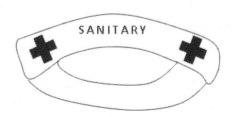

The Faxer separated the band from the bubble with a unique instrument. The bubble was a small spherical object. It looked like this:

The spherical nature of the bubble was nearly perfect in form. Otherwise, it may have resembled something like an apple. An apple looks like this:

Had it looked like an apple, people could have associated it more with knowledge as if it had come from the tree of knowledge in the Garden of Eden. It hadn't come from such a mythical place. It had come from the mind of a flawed human many years in the past.

Wearing special gloves, the Faxer carried the single bubble over to the Past Psyche Penetration machine. The machine was known as the PPP. The future seemed to like acronyms too. It was a machine for sending the bubble into the past to the psyche of someone. It couldn't be just any someone. They had to be alive within 10 years of the death of the person whose thought was in the bubble. The receiver's psyche also had to be structured similarly to the person who originally thought the thought that was in the bubble now. The Faxer had to do a lot of research to find just the right person.

. . .

It was the inaugural sending of a thought to the past. Many dignitaries stood in an adjacent room and watched anxiously through a two-way mirror as the Faxer prepared to send "Lazzaro 1" to its Transistor. The Faxer slowly and carefully walked to the PPP. Thought bubbles were fragile, and one misstep and a drop would destroy something that had survived 8 World Wars.

The PPP was large and took up much of the room. It was shaped like a pyramid. An opening about two thirds of the way up housed a socket in which the bubble was initially placed. The machine looked like this:

The Faxer climbed the nine steps placed next to the PPP as to reach the socket. The various dignitaries in the adjacent room gasped as the Faxer stumbled on the third step. The Faxer recovered quickly, and the bubble was safe. After placing the bubble in the socket, the Faxer walked back down the steps. At the base of the pyramid were a number of buttons. The Faxer pressed one.

The bubble in the socket was covered by a metal dome and dropped slowly into the internal works at the base of the machine. Inside, a specially designed rod slammed into the bubble releasing the thought. The thought exploded in all directions and looked like a star shining. If someone could have looked into the machine, the process would have looked like this:

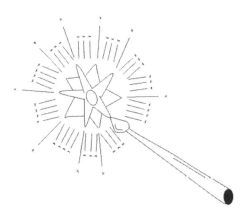

The PPP duplicated the encrypted thought and resealed one version in another bubble. That bubble would end up at the base of the machine to be stored away again. The other version would find no home in a bubble. It would be sent to the top of the pyramid. When the whole thought arrived at the top, a green button would light up telling the Faxer it was ready to be sent to the past.

The green button lit up showing the inaugural thought was waiting to be sent. The Faxer pressed the final button of the process, and the eye at the top of the pyramid shined. When the PPP had sent the entire message, the eye went dark. Moments later, a book appeared on the nearby shelf. The Faxer rushed to the shelf to open the book. Opening the book, the Faxer saw, "lo." Coincidentally, it was the same inaugural message as the one sent on the Internet more than a millennium before. Shaking his head, the Faxer knew something had gone wrong.

...

David Klein was a young, gay man living in rural Mississippi. He was 19 years old. David was careful with who he let know his secret. To be gay in rural America was nearly a death wish. Only his boyfriend knew, and no one else. Some of the people who didn't know would care less what he did privately. The other people who didn't know were scared of cooties, moral decay, or their own inner voice telling them that they preferred the same sex. People were strange creatures, but some of them were so scared of the "gays" that they would bully, ostracize, or even murder someone over it.

The inaugural thought bubble slammed into David's psyche. It rearranged his thinking like a tornado adjusts the layout of a trailer park. Pain shot through his body, and he shook as if being electrocuted. The bubble bombarded his psyche with words, but it was leveling his synaptic junctions like the Allied bombers had done to Dresden. Stumbling as he fought against the pain, he raced to his desk. His computer was on. He had started to write a paper for his college course on anthropology. The page staring back at him had only the title. Shaking violently, he struggled to push the backspace button enough times to delete the title. He could feel a need to write and get out what was within. With great effort, he placed his fingers on the home keys to type. His right ring finger shook and depressed the L key, then the O key. He couldn't do it. He couldn't get this thing out that was within him. The door to the closet of his mind would not let its contents be seen.

A single tear fell from his clover green eye. It looked like this:

David stood up and knocked over his desk chair. He clinched his teeth in an attempt to fight off the pain. It didn't really help. Nothing seemed to help. The pain was just too unbearable. Sweating, shaking, and mumbling, David went to the closet to get the rope from his repelling gear. He made a noose and hung himself. So it goes.

After his death, people would find out he was gay and assume that he committed suicide because of it. They were wrong, of course. The truth was that while David's psyche was structured almost identically to Joe Lazzaro's, it was not even remotely as perverse. It was the perversity of the heterosexual Lazzaro that had killed the homosexual Klein. So it goes.

•••

Vonnegut awoke to a knock on his door. He was still a little groggy as he got up from the hard cot.

"124C…124C," a voice behind the door kept repeating.

"Yes, yes, I'm up," Vonnegut mumbled back. He walked to the sink to slash water on his face and fully wake up. He felt exhausted having spent nearly the whole night thinking up this story.

The door opened as Vonnegut was wiping the water from his face with a towel.

"124C?" the guard said in a half questioning, half asserting tone.

Vonnegut walked over to the guard and placed his right hand on the guard's shoulder.

"Who else would I be?" Vonnegut said with a smile.

"Sir, it's your turn," the guard stated returning Vonnegut's smile.

After walking down the hallway, outside, into another building, down another hallway, into an elevator that took them some 30 floors underground, and down another long hallway, they reached their destination.

Waiting outside the lab door was Heath. He had a grin on his face.

"Good luck," the director said with a hint of sarcasm.

Heath knew that they had had to institutionalize a few of the earlier participants because the TT process had driven them to insanity. He was quietly hoping that it would do the same to Vonnegut.

The guard opened the door for Vonnegut. Hearing the tone of Heath, Vonnegut changed his mind about apologizing to Heath for his outburst yesterday. Vonnegut paused a moment and considered replying with his quick wit to Heath. He decided it was not worth the time and turned to enter the lab. As a peace offering, Vonnegut instead offered his hand to shake. Heath took it. A handshake looks like this:

The first thing Vonnegut noticed in the lab was the oversized, 50 foot flag hanging on the back wall. The room was huge, and it seemed as if the ceiling reached the sky. The American flag hung on that back wall in honor of all the poor taxpayers whose money had been sunk into the TT project and the government who had believed in the scientists' prognostications. The flag looked like this:

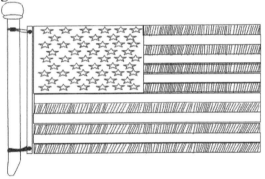

The second object Vonnegut noticed was the TT machine itself. It sat squarely in the middle of the room and looked like a torture device. The TT machine looked like this:

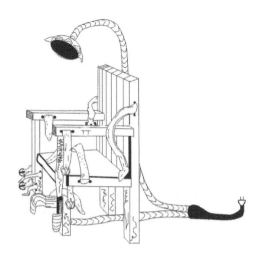

Vonnegut fought back the urge to say, "You really want *me* to sit in *that*?" but he kept quiet. He knew it was the only means to get his last novel done, and he was determined. The numerous technicians in the room kept giving Vonnegut instructions. He followed every one and ended up seated in the TT machine with the halo placed over his curly, grey-haired head.

"When will it start?" Vonnegut asked. His one and only question after entering the lab.

One of the scientists pointed to a clock directly in front of Vonnegut.

"Approximately 2 minutes," scientists said, "when the big hand hits the two." The clock looked like this:

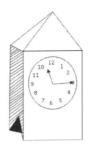

Why they had such an old-fashion clock in a room full of the most advanced technologies was beyond Vonnegut's comprehension. The hand moved to the two. Vonnegut began his last work.

Vonnegut, Slaughter House Five, Tralfamadorians' response to Billy Pilgrim.

Like a rattlesnake, the TT machine hissed and rattled as it began storing his thoughts. A rattlesnake looked like this:

FIVE

Wearing his newest Armani suit, Kevin Dewayne Roland used his remote to turn off his 52 inch HDTV. Companies didn't just use acronyms for themselves but also their products. He got up from his leather, desk chair and walked out of his home office. His assets were substantial. Rare artworks, multiple mansions, exotic cars, and aged alcohol were among his many possessions. His parents would never have imagined that he would find himself in such luxurious circumstances. Well, not his biological parents, that is. Roland was born at the corner of Skid Row and Destitution Avenue. One of the signs looked like this:

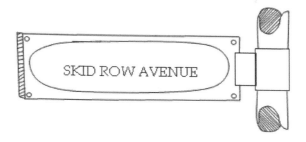

Roland headed to his mancave. To call it a mancave was an understatement, it was more like a batcave. The batcave was the secret hideaway of the billionaire, Bruce Wayne, whose alter ego was Batman. Both Bruce Wayne and Batman were fictitious though, characters created by the writing of Bill Finger and the artwork of Bob Kane. Batman was a good guy. Roland was not.

...

Evelyn was born Merry Hope Glitche. It was a name she rarely used anymore though. Evelyn's parents were part of the working poor in Ilium, New York. They had little to their name except for hope. Having finally conceived a child after numerous failed attempts, they had wanted a name that would not only be unique but would display the one thing they owned, hope.

At 28, Evelyn had anything but hope. Her caring parents had died nearly 20 years ago. So it goes. They had left her nothing. Their hope must have followed them to their taxpayer supported graves. Evelyn was an orphan and placed in foster care. Although they were not physically abusive, her foster parents devoted almost no time to the 12 kids they had taken in. The kids ran amuck. Evelyn was skipping school as early as seventh grade. She met her first boyfriend while taking one of her many breaks from her education. He was 19, and she was 13. Her boyfriend could give her freedom because he had a car and buy her some of the clothes and accessories she desired. She could give him sex. Both felt they were getting the better end of the arrangement. And so on.

...

Judy Thompson and Hilda Hurley told me a funny story the other day. Linda, who no one likes, has a son who is quite promiscuous. That boy gets around, if you know what I mean. The boy tells his mom everything, and she is not one to keep secrets. One night her son went out to a nightclub to drink and find if he could add to his substantial number of conquests. He met a woman who I can't remember her name. Anyway, he seduces her as playboys do and ends up going home with her. They have sex. Cuddling close to the woman, he sneezes and apologizes that he has allergies. The woman tells him that there are tissues in the top drawer of the nightstand. He opens the nightstand to get a tissue and sees a picture.

Taking the picture out, Linda's son asks, "Is this your husband?"

"No," the woman giggles.

Still nervous, he asks, "Your boyfriend?"

"I'm all yours," she says, "there is no one else."

"Really?", he says relieved, "Then, who is this?"

"Me, before the operation," the woman clarifies.

Serves that boy right. He shouldn't be doing what he's doing.

···

I think the Faxer had accidently sent me the wrong thought bubble. Lucky for me, my psyche was similar to the bubble's thinker, otherwise, I may have not been able to take it like poor David Klein. In fact, the Faxer has sent me the thought bubble of Karen Von Gleiss, the only TT participant, other than Merriam Beauveaux, who knew Judy and Hilda. Human error must still exist in the future.

···

But to continue:

As is too common for people in Evelyn's shoes, tragedy would pay a visit. After six months of unprotected sex, Evelyn and her boyfriend won the lottery. They were pregnant. Well, they weren't, she was. She was still only 13, and her boyfriend was nearing his 20th birthday. Not but a couple years back, she still thought that storks delivered babies. One doing so would look like this:

Evelyn's boyfriend was smart enough to know that he was committing statutory rape, but he didn't care. He also knew that the pregnancy would expose that cruelty.

Evelyn's boyfriend convinced her to get an abortion. The landmark case of Roe v Wade making abortion legal, standardized, and accessible was still many years away. They would have to either do it themselves or find someone to do it. After considering using a coat hanger, they decided that they should trust getting it right to someone with experience. With time, Evelyn's boyfriend found such a person. Dr. Landon Richards had been a pediatrician for eight years before losing his medical license. He was addicted to numerous illegal drugs. When they met with him, he was as high as a new credit card's interest rate.

Richards performed Evelyn's abortion. It would be her first, but it would not be her last. She would have five more over the coming years. Each was a separate man's contribution to her life. Richards took care of all of them with the exception of one. He was incarcerated at that time.

...

Roland entered the five digit code to his secret mancave, said "fuck niggers" to clear the voice activation security, and leaned in for a retinal scan. The sealed door opened. He promptly stepped through the threshold and closed the door behind him.

Roland hated homosexuals, and he was a secret and significant financial contributor to the Westboro Baptist Church. As a somewhat recent convert to neo-Nazism, Roland also hated everyone who was not White. A large Nazi flag adorned the far wall. It looked like this:

On an adjacent wall was an Iron Cross. The Iron Cross looked like this:

Roland had accepted the radical ideology of neo-Nazism as his most recent drug. He had had a number of drugs in his past. Some were objects. Others were experiences. He walked over to one of his priced possessions. It was desk that had once been owned by Joseph Goebbels. Goebbels was listed in Hitler's will as his successor. Walking pass the desk, Roland slid his had across the top. It was a common habit of his. He thought it would bring more inspiration about how to terrorize chinks, niggers, hymies, spicks, and gays.

He glanced around some of the items in the room seeking to draw inspiration. His eyes quickly scanned passed the large area in the corner of the room devoted to cosmetics, makeup, and costumes. Roland paused on the wall near the cosmetics. An enlarged copy of an old sign from Shepardstown hung on the wall. It looked like this:

NIGGER! THIS IS SHEPHARDSTOWN. GOD CAN'T HELP YOU IF THE SUN EVER SETS ON YOU HERE!

Next to the poster, Roland had had another poster crafted for the space. The frames were identical in size. The second poster housed an enlarged copy of the book cover of Vonnegut's collection of stories called Welcome to the Monkey House. Roland had never read the book, but he liked the idea of comparing African Americans to monkeys. He always took the juxtaposition of the Shepardstown sign and the book cover as artistic genius on his part.

With all his money, Roland had become bored by all the luxuries it provided. He had gone through various stages as to how to use his vast resources. First, he spent on extravagant items like cars and homes and world trips. He still felt the whole, the gap, within him that those things could not fill. Roland imagined that his money would give him that spark of being alive. He wanted it, but could not find it in extravagant items. Any rich person could have those things.

Second, Roland thought that sex, love, or both would fill the absence within him. He dated supermodels and actresses and splurged on them with no reservation. One of the supermodels had a rare kitten that she treated like a baby. Roland bought her a special Cat's Cradle with closely constructed bars that were four feet tall made of titanium. The poor kitten could never escape its bed.

Some of the women fell in love with Roland, but he was not designed to return real love. His quest to fill his desire continued to remain unfulfilled.

Roland's third stage of fulfilling his desire came as a philanthropist. He donated large sums to various charities and won numerous awards. This, too, did not fulfill him.

Thinking about his philanthropy days, Roland walked to a corner of his mancave. A pile of items rested there. Grabbing a rolled up poster, he unrolled it. It was from the 19th annual Ilium Shakespeare Festival. The poster had two masks on it. One symbolized tragedy and looked like this:

The other symbolized comedy. It looked like this:

Roland flung the poster to the side. He dug in a box and found two buttons. One looked like this:

And the other looked like this:

They were identical. Roland had a ton of them. He tossed both back into the box.

The final stage of Roland's spending was the one that he had found joy in. He used his money to get away with crime. Not just any crime. He had already done White collar crime like fraud and embezzlement. No, it had to be blue collar crime. How many billionaires could do that? he thought. He had already done a few blue collar crimes, and he went to his desk, sat down, and enjoyed the nostalgia of those atrocities.

•••

Evelyn was kicked out of her foster parents' house on her 18th birthday. She had little education and no skills. The only skill she believed she was good at was sex. After only a week of being homeless and taking food from a shelter, she met a pimp who called himself Deadeye Dick. Old Deadeye knew fresh talent and helplessness when he saw it. Highlighting the money-making potential like an infomercial, Old Deadeye had Evelyn working the streets that night. In fact, it was that night that Merry Hope Glitche became known simply as Evelyn. The Merry was gone, the Hope was gone, and that which gave her a history, a family history to be specific, was erased. Deadeye Dick said Evelyn was a much more marketable name. Johns surely would not want to have sex with a woman because of her name. Johns were the generic name given to any man seeking a prostitute. While Evelyn's name mattered, according to Old Deadeye, the men's names really didn't. Only the money they had mattered.

•••

Roland sat at his desk in his mancave and reflected on his past exploits. After his use of his resources for objects, women, and philanthropy, he had felt no meaning to his existence. That changed when he had an epiphany. He would commit crimes. Getting away with them gave him a rush like no previous object, woman, or act could do.

A few years back, Roland committed his first, blue collar crime. He did not plan it as well as his more recent escapades, but he had not gotten caught. Before deciding to take the path of crime, Roland shifted his priorities slightly. He had told himself that the three people most important for success were a good lawyer, a successful financial advisor, and a personal accountant. That had worked when objects, women, and charity ruled the day. But, determined to get away with crimes, Roland employed a black market surgeon, a person skilled in forgery, and a cosmetic artist. He still kept the lawyer, financial advisor, and accountant retained, but he knew he would also need these three new employees. The surgeon was a precaution in case one of his exploits ended up causing him bodily harm. Roland had employed the forgery specialist to obtain a variety of identities. So far, Roland had used the services of the cosmetic artist the most. The cosmetic artist had previously been employed in Hollywood to change the stature, physical features, and overall look of actors and actresses. Roland always disguised himself when he ventured to one of his escapades. His identity was a lie, but he knew he needed it to not get caught. Like you, I hate being lied to.

Many autumns ago, Roland had the cosmetic artist convert him into a handsome, 28 year old veteran. His fake scraggly beard and colored contacts as well as a body suit that added pseudo-muscles to his upper body were quite convincing. He dressed in camouflage pants and a white t-shirt. In the pants pocket was a case that held a metal of valor that Roland had purchased. It was one of the only real things he had as a prop and looked like this:

Roland used the valor metal as bait for the trap he was about to conduct. In his other pant pocket, he placed his new wallet. A fake driver's license, insurance card, business card, multiple fake credit cards filled the wallet. The only thing not fake in the wallet was the cash. But, Roland had plenty of that, so he didn't need to go into counterfeiting.

It was the first Friday of September, and the sun had set. In the guise of Sgt. John Little, Roland obtained a room at the no-tell-motel, the Traveler's Paradise, on the outer edge of Ilium. He had driven there in his beetle. It looked like this:

It was the most inconspicuous vehicle he owned. He had removed the plates from it and placed a "plates applied for" sign in the back window.

After checking into the Traveler's Paradise, Roland took a bag from the car to prepare the room for the night. Brass knuckles, knives, rope, a ball gag, and other items filled the bag. He hid them throughout the room. He was energized with anticipation.

At 10pm, Roland got in his beetle and drove to the only gay bar in town, the Clair Du Lune Lounge. Its promotion was single banner over its doorway. The banner looked like this:

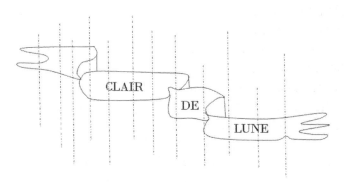

Three hours later, after seducing a young naïve gay male with his fake war stories and metal of valor, Roland was back at the motel, but he was not alone.

The gay male, with thoughts of a sexual encounter, had come with him. The poor naïve male was tied to a chair in the center of the room. Roland had sucker punched him with the brass knuckles as the boy was getting undressed. The young boy had recently moved to Ilium in an attempt to forget the harsh memory of his ex-lover, David Klein, who had committed suicide. He slouched, tied to a chair, barely conscious. Roland placed the ball gag on the unsuspecting male to make sure he made no noise. He turned on the television to give the appearance to those who would pass outside that nothing peculiar was transpiring in the room.

After whipping the boy with a bullwhip several times causing his bright red blood to drip from his back, Roland grinned. Now came the part Roland had anticipated all night. He placed all his items back in the bag because he knew he would be leaving soon. All, but two, that is. Roland plugged in the tattoo gun and readied the pink, black, and purple inks he had brought. He took a ready-made stencil with the word "gay" on it and placed it on the young man's forehead. Roland had decided that stenciling the letters would be safer so no clever forensic scientist could decode his handwriting. With the word "gay" now tattooed in pink and outlined in black on the young man's forehead, Roland moved to his last task. He took a larger stencil with the word "FAGGOT" on it. The tattoo gun hummed as Roland meticulously transcribed the word in purple ink on the unconscious man's chest. Happy and finished, he packed the gun and ink in his bag and left the room.

The young man would survive the incident. At least physically, he would. His cheekbone that the brass knuckles had shattered and the deep lacerations on his back from the whipping were reconstructed and fixed by two surgeons working pro bono. With help from a local victim's fund, he would have the two tattoos removed. But the memory of that night would haunt him for the rest of his days.

Roland returned from his nostalgic daydream. Sitting at his desk and facing his computer, he turned the computer on to look at the value of his assets and see if his secret shipment had arrived at his hidden warehouse address.

...

After working for Deadeye Dick for a number of months, Evelyn still had little to her name. The income she brought in from the various sexual favors she provided was significant, but, like all pimps, Old Deadeye got the lion's share. Evelyn didn't understand why she needed a pimp. He didn't do anything for her. Of course, she never told him that. She had seen too many other prostitutes beaten by him to voice her thoughts.

Like a middle class family saving for their child's college education, she tucked away a little money at a time. Unlike the other girls working for Deadeye, Evelyn did not spend her money on drugs to dull the pain of her life's experience. She was strong willed and thought drugs where the crutches of the weak. Her lack of drug addiction had made Deadeye suspicious. She was running out of time to have enough money to make her break.

...

Roland's computer booted quickly. He had spared no expense on it. Looking over his assets, Roland found that he had a lost small percent of his wealth in his investments. It was not a significant amount given the vastness of his portfolio, but he watched his money like a mother looks after her newborn. Tomorrow, he decided, he would call his financial consultant and ask what had happened.

Changing screens, he found that his shipment had arrived. He would plan and execute his next criminal act over the coming days.

Roland sat back in his chair and reflected on another of his past exploits. There were a number of them, but this one often brought a smile to his face when he thought about it. He had harmed a standing US Senator and gotten away with it.

About eight months ago, Roland had been watching the news accounts of an interview with Senator Aiken Todd. He was a 60 year old who represented a Midwestern state. In the interview Todd had made clear that only legitimate rape created children. All other rape was illegitimate. It seems, according to Todd, the female body had a way to shut down and keep unwanted sperm from fertilizing their eggs. Roland was so disgusted by the comments that he vowed to himself to take action. Todd was White and the only non-minority to garner Roland's violent acts, but Roland felt he had to make an exception.

Using an array of his disguises, Roland searched the black market trying to locate the proper assistant. After a week of nonstop searching, he found Tank Rizo. Rizo was ex-military and built as his name suggested. Unlike Roland, he was a family man and took odd criminal jobs to help support his wife and five kids. He came highly recommended because he followed directions well, performed what was asked, and never spoke of any of his dealings. He loved his family and did not want to be a Jailbird or be murdered by an associate, so he made sure to keep a good reputation among thieves, killers, extortionists, rapists, and drug lords.

In the guise of Mrs. Katie Holiday, Roland met with Rizo and discussed his plan. Roland had specifically selected the name Katie because it was a name used during his childhood to ridicule him since his initials were KD. Kevin Dewayne became KD or Katie. Rolands' Mrs. Holiday costume was complete with a voice modulator to make him sound like a woman. The modulator was embedded in a broach and was designed by the Japanese inventor, Zenji Hiroguchi.

"So, could you do it?" Holiday asked in her soft, feminine voice.

"Hell, depends on the money, I guess," replied Rizo.

Money was not an issue for Roland, but he had to play his cards right. If the offer was too grandiose, Rizo may think it untrue. If too low, Roland would miss hiring the perfect assistant.

"Maybe, you should tell me what you think it's worth," stated Holiday.

Rizo did not like to negotiate. He only wanted to know what he could earn.

"No, you tell me," Rizo stated sternly.

Roland leaned forward and in a soft voice said, "200,000."

"Well…", Rizo said drawing it out. It was a tactic he had learned from working in the black market economy for so many years. Anyone wanting you to commit a crime was going to gain from it in some way, and they never gave you their best offer first.

"Okay," Roland said, taking the bait, "250,000."

"Deal," asserted Rizo, extending his hand to shake on it. Two hundred and fifty thousand dollars was ten times as much as Rizo made all year in his "day job," and this job would be done in a weekend. He couldn't pass it up. Rizo told himself he was doing it for his family.

Mrs. Katie Holiday shook on it. The arrangement's details were worked out. They met at the airport, Holiday paid Rizo half up front, and they flew to Senator Todd's home state on the coming weekend.

…

Two odd things came from the dealing of Roland, as Holiday, and Rizo. First, it was ironic that Roland hated homosexuals with a passion, yet he felt completely comfortable wearing lipstick, eye liner, and rouge, in a skirt, blouse, and high heels. He was oblivious of the irony. Second, Rizo would launder the money and use it to create a college fund for his five kids. Four decades later, Rizo's oldest daughter would win the Nobel Peace Prize.

…

The thing was:

After arriving in Senator Aiken Todd's Midwestern state, Roland and Rizo kidnapped the Senator. Well, Rizo really did it. He simply drugged him and, then, placed him in the trunk of his rental car. That was the first half of his job. Rizo headed to meet up with Mrs. Holiday. Once they met up, they had to act fast since a missing politician often drew attention. Just ask Governor Mark Sanford about his hiking of the Appalachian Trail.

Driving for about two hours, Rizo reached the abandoned building in the middle of nowhere. Mrs. Holiday was already there, waiting.

Rizo carried Todd's unconscious body like a sack of potatoes over his shoulder. Setting the Senator facedown on a small, cold, metal table, Rizo prepared for the second job he had been paid for. He stripped the Senator's lower body naked, cuffed each of his wrists to their corresponding table leg, and cuffed his ankles to the other legs. The Senator was spread out as if being drawn and quartered. Rizo lifted the Senator's head from the front edge of the table and placed a blindfold on him. The smelling salts were brought, and the Senator regained consciousness.

"You're gonna be sorry for this. Do you know who I am?" the Senator said defiantly and arrogantly.

"Why do you think we chose you?" Roland said in the voice of Katie Holliday.

With that said, Rizo began to sodomize the poor Senator from a Midwestern state.

"No, please, no," he cried, but it was in vain.

The climax came, and Todd felt warm degradation fill him. He was broken, abused, shattered, with no ounce of dignity and only shame, depression, and guilt to fill its void. Todd had been raped. Todd never got pregnant from the rape, so we can assume it was not legitimate. His body was designed to shut down any attempt at pregnancy.

···

Roland returned from his devious daydream and decided to locate his souvenir from that fateful night. Scrounging through a box in the far recesses of his mancave, he found the Senator's underwear. The underwear looked like this:

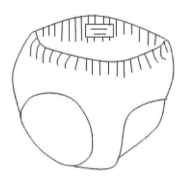

Roland knew they could be used as evidence against him, but he felt confident in the security system guarding his trusted mancave. He had already destroyed all records and traces of the Katie Holiday identity. Roland believed nothing and no one could stop him.

In fact, Todd, like many rape victims, never reported the crime. Like the naïve young gay man who had been seduced to a hotel room by a charming military hero, the Senator would never be the same.

···

Listen:
Evelyn had enough money to make it for a short time on her own without Deadeye Dick. She just didn't

know how to leave him and not be tracked down and beaten like other girls had been who attempted to cut him out of the money. As luck would have it, Deadeye Dick overdosed on prescription drugs. So it goes.

Free from the tyranny of Deadeye Dick, Evelyn adjusted her work habits. She worked the streets less and less but prowled the internet looking for Johns. Evelyn became more sophisticated and referred to Johns as clients. She also bought a nice, formal dress to serve as an escort to wealthy men who where not simply looking for sex. The money was steadily coming in.

One night, while working the lounge of an upscale hotel in Ilium, Evelyn met James Wait. He told her he was an investment banker and attempted to con her. Wait was a crafty con-artist, but Evelyn had interacted with so many men that she was immune to his Hocus Pocus. Using her sensuality and developed craft, she coaxed him into a sexual soirée for the next hour at a rate of $500. He never stood a chance.

Each would give the other an unexpected gift that night. Wait would give Evelyn a child. Evelyn would give Wait crabs. Crabs was a slang name for pubic lice. With greater hygiene practices, biologist feared that crabs were becoming an endangered species or even faced extinction. A single pubic louse looked like this:

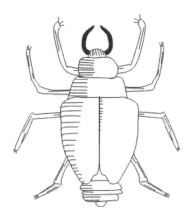

After Evelyn's six abortions and three miscarriages, the new life growing in her womb would end up making her a mother.

···

Having spent the rest of the day reflecting on all his past blue collar crime and longing to commit another, Roland headed to bed. Tomorrow, he thought, would be a long day.

Roland woke early and headed to the hidden warehouse to pick up his secret package. It was a box of castor beans. The castor beans were cheap and easy to attain. However, he didn't want them being traced back to him, so he paid extra and had them delivered to a fake name. The beans housed a significantly potent toxin called ricin. Roland planned to extract the poison and use it for his next exploit. It would end up being the first time he himself would kill another person.

···

As Evelyn's babybump became more noticeable, she was forced to work the streets more and the internet less. She did not give up on earning some cash through the internet entirely. There was a select group of men who would pay extra to have sex with a pregnant woman. Evelyn always thought such men fantasized about a menange a trois or threesome with a mother and daughter. She never told any that the child was a boy.

Late on a cool summer night, Evelyn began working her block. Her feet were swollen, and her back ached. Evelyn stopped to steady herself at a street sign. The east-west road was called Destitution Avenue. The north-south road was Skid Row. She shook her head. The city council had decided to re-label the streets in the poor area of Ilium to caution travelers who may have wandered there on accident.

The pain in her feet and back as well as worry about the health of the baby distracted Evelyn from the fact that she had started contracts nearly an hour ago. Looking up at the street signs, she felt a powerful and painful contraction that took her mind off her feet and back. Evelyn moaned and sat down on the cold concrete sidewalk. Trying to gather herself, the next contraction hit her like a tidal wave. She had no watch and didn't know how far apart the two contractions had been, but she knew they were close. Evelyn knew she had to get to a hospital and soon.

...

Walking near the corner of Skid Row and Destitution Avenue was Dwayne, the uncle of the meth-making, skateboarding, fraternity boy, Brody O'Malley. Dwayne was dealing weed and LSD. Drug dealers seemed to like acronyms too. Business was slow. He pulled out his pack of Pall Malls and lit a cigarette. Dwayne only smoked them because Santa Clause had once endorsed them. He took a long drag. The cool buzz of the marijuana-laced smoke relaxed him.

He heard a woman moan in pain diagonally across the intersection. Having nothing better to do, he decided to investigate.

"Help," Evelyn shouted as she saw Dwayne approaching.

"What's wrong?" he asked.

"I'm pregnant," she said, "and going into…" Evelyn would have said labor but the contraction washed over her.

She didn't need to finish the sentence, Dwayne understood what was happening.

"Get me to a hospital," she proclaimed.

"Uh, I, uh, don't have a car."

"Damnit, call.." Another wave of pain bore down on her. The contractions were close, and there was no time to get to the proper medical facilities.

"You have to do it," she said.

Dwayne didn't want to get involved. Evelyn convinced him that there were no other options.

There on the corner of Skid Row and Destitution, Dwayne helped a stranger have her son. For his assistance, Evelyn would give her son the middle name Dwayne. The birth certificate would list no father, since Evelyn was unsure which of the countless men had donated his sperm to its conception. And it would read Kevin Dwayne Glitche.

...

Evelyn would raise Kevin for a year with the help of the Our God is Holier than Yours Church of Ilium. She knew, however, that she could not give him the life he deserved. Evelyn put him up for adoption.

A childless, young, middle class couple named Larry and Rita Roland adopted little Kevin. They raised him until he was ten, and legally changed his last name to match theirs. Unlike Evelyn's parents, Larry and Rita not only had hope but luck. When their son, their only child, was nine, the Rolands won the largest Powerball lottery jackpot in US history. Six months later, they died in a tragic accident on their way to pick up Kevin at baseball practice. Being their only living relative, the Roland's entire estate went to Kevin. By the time Kevin's 18th birthday came and he had access to all the funds, they had tripled in value. He was set for life.

...

That's right, you could call Roland a son of a whore, and you wouldn't be lying. Like you, I hate being lied to.

SIX

Listen:

Since I do not know how educated you will be, Vonnegut's thought bubble began, you should attend a few university lectures to better understand all the shit in your world. I'd recommend Harvard if it still exists, he added. I didn't want to go back to school. I had spent enough time in college to earn credits worthy of an astrophysicist at Los Alamos. I just couldn't get enough of them in an area so that the school could confer me with a degree in a specific area. Classroom learning was my Achilles' heel. My time in college had taught me that Achilles was a great warrior who the gods dipped in magic potion to make him invincible. The divine creatures were erudite enough to be able to make the magic potion but dumb enough to not realize that the place they touched to dip him would not be covered in the magic sauce. Just like Alice Winner who wanted a picture of a cute, forest animal, Achilles' weakness was his heel.

...

I tried to get out of attending college again. I waited hoping that the dreaded consequences of the thought bubble would subside. They didn't. The bubbles and Vonnegut had control of me. I was a machine for printing his words, and I had to obey the directions or suffer the consequences, which were too unbearable.

In the Fall, Harvard had a special "Check out us" program where idiots like me could pay a small sum of money and attend any three lectures we wanted.

It became confusing for professors there because they couldn't keep track of who was a student and who was an educational tourist. It was the only Fall that they had the program, so I was lucky. It was serendipitous that I should live near Boston where Harvard is. Then again, most things in novels are serendipitous.

···

The first lecture I attended was an evening class on Lacanian psychoanalysis. Lacan was a French psychologist who reframed Freud's sexual perversions into technical jibberish for people who wanted to sound smart. The class was taught by a Professor Levin Lovejoy. It was a large lecture, so I sat near the back. For most of the lecture, Lovejoy addressed something called jouissance. I could care less about jouissance. I had my eye on a lovely, young student who was one row in front of me and to the right. She was stunning. Her red dress accentuated her curved form, and her light brown hair was up displaying the beautiful lines of her neck. She was sensuality in its purest form. Her name was Blossom Priest. Just as I began to fantasize about this green-eyed beauty, my thoughts were interrupted. Lovejoy was nearly shouting the word "jouissance." Jouissance this, jouissance that, he kept saying. Ok, ok, I thought, Lacan likes jouissance. Can you please keep your jouissance to yourself so I can fantasize about this beautiful woman before me?

···

While I didn't have a college degree, I read significantly. My figurative jouissance came from learning new things on my own. I didn't really like someone telling me what everything in the world meant.

Roland was different. He got pure jouissance from creating suffering and pain in minorities or those who supported minority groups.

...

Blossom Priest left the psychology class when it ended. I watched her walk away without asking her out. I was fearless is in some ways. Having been scuba diving, surfing, skydiving, and hang gliding, I never cowered to a challenge. I even won the New Eastern US middleweight boxing title for my region. At the next level, I had been KO'd though. Sports liked acronyms just like drug dealers, businesses, and products. But women, women were another creature all together. It took a lot for me to have the nerve to approach them. I told myself that if I saw her again, I would surely ask her out.

...

My next course was the following day. It was an early class, and I was no early bird. I set my unique alarm clock as to make certain I didn't miss it. The alarm clock was manufactured in China. I had bought it at a thrift shop after hearing the song about thrift shopping by Macklemore. Media has such an impact on people. The first time the alarm ever went off, I found why it had been given to the thrift shop. It seems that the alarm was supposed to be programmed to say, "Why? Oh, you know why. It's time to get up." Because of faulting engineering and cheap electronics, it simply repeated the first three words endlessly, pausing after each three-letter sequence. Thus, it sounded like it was spelling a word endlessly:

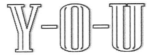

Turning off the annoying alarm that I had gotten used to, I rushed to shower and clean up to go to my second lecture.

I barely arrived to the class on time. To my surprise, Blossom Priest was there too. I wanted to sit near her. Her sensuality was radiant. Others could feel it, it seemed. There was not an empty chair within with three seats of her. I sat as near as I could, but it did not feel near enough.

...

Professor Margaret Twane entered the classroom. She was an older lady who wore her glasses on a chain. The spectacles themselves hung down near her bosom. Dr. Twane looked like a stereotypical librarian, but she was far from soft-spoken.

"Today," she took a long pause, "we will examine the various literary symbols, the symbolism you could say, in great works of literature." She emphasized the word literature by not only punctuating each syllable but by gesturing as she did.

She was a well-established scholar in literary circles. She was not a very organized teacher, however. Dr. Twane never liked the organized linear plot structure and taught her course as if it was haplessly meandering. Life outside the book followed few rules, so why should my class have structure? She would often profess.

"Trains, and especially train tracks, are a sign of what within a text?" she asked the class.

The professor waited. No brave soul attempted to answer.

With no hands to call on, Dr. Twane randomly called on someone. She selected Blossom.

Blossom stammered, "Uh, well, uhm….." She was nervous. Even though she was quite intelligent, Blossom was still adjusting to English as it was not her first language. She seemed embarrassed.

I rushed to her aid and shouted, "Progress. They show progress."

"Sure," she said condescendingly, "anyone could say progress, and progress can be used for the answer of any new technology's symbolism in a novel or story."

I didn't mind being wrong. I felt that I was right to come to Blossom's defense.

…

Many people say, "If at first you don't succeed, try, try again."

Cynics say, "If at first you don't succeed, quit so you don't look like a fool."

Comedians say, "If at first you don't succeed, skydiving is probably not for you."

I was one who didn't worry about success. I had been skydiving. I didn't do it to succeed. I did it to *see if* I would succeed.

…

But to continue:

Professor Twane shook her head with discontent.

Putting her palms facing each other but with her hands slightly apart, she asked, "But, tracks, focus on train tracks, what, by god, do they highlight?"

A brave, young lady near the front raised her hand.

"Yes?" Dr. Twane said, nodding to the young lady.

"Parallelism. The tracks are always parallel, so they mean that there is some parallel in the story."

It was not the answer that the professor desperately desired.

"No," the professor stated abruptly, "it is destiny."

Dr. Twane went on about the fact that trains can only go the direction in which the tracks are laid. Characters on the train are following their destiny, going to the only place to which they could.

The literary expert went on to tell the class that the device was used in many stories. Tolstoy's "Anna Karenina," Christie's "Murder on the Orient Express," Drieser's "Sister Carrie," Hawthorne's "Celestial Railroad," and countless others made the list.

"Most literature that incorporates the train as a symbol is modern," she added.

"I do not mean 'modern' like 'new', as many of you are surely to think, if you are anything like previously classes. I mean 'modern' compared to postmodern."

She continued to explain the difference between modernity and postmodernity. Modernity was structured, rational, linear, believed in metanarrative, and has a sense of closure. Postmodernity sometimes lacked structure, was emotive, often circular, would undermine metanarrative, and may appear open ended.

"I am not aware of any clearly postmodern text that employs the train," Dr. Twane stated, "but Vonnegut's Slaughterhouse Five overlaps the line between modernity and postmodernity. And it has trains."

The class ended.

Blossom had waited by the door for me to thank me. I would have met her then, but I was held after by the teacher. Dr. Twane wanted to reprimand me for interfering with her likely interrogation.

"You are not a student, you are a guest," she repeated endlessly as if she had no other words for her disappointment.

"Yeah, I know," I endlessly repeated back.

Needing to get to her next class, Blossom left. I would not see her for some time.

•••

Given the class, it appears to me that the postmodern Man was simply the enlightened Man without the mystique. I was postmodern before I knew I was postmodern. And I'll be postmodern after I realize I'm not. Then again, maybe I wouldn't be.

•••

Some days passed before my third and final class on my cheap, educational tour of Harvard. My final class would be an introduction to philosophy and was taught by Professor Timothy Locke.

Excited because it was the last class I would need to attend and because I had read a significant amount of philosophy in the past, I headed to the lecture.

Dr. Locke began the class with a crude drawing he wrote on the white board. It looked like this:

Pointing to the image, he said, "We all start life coming through the same door."

He continued.

"As Cornell West has said, we are born in the funk between piss and shit," Locke stated. Of course, what Locke didn't tell us was that West had appropriated the idea popularized by Yeats.

> *A woman can be proud and stiff*
> *When on love intent;*
> *But Love has pitched his mansion in*
> *The place of excrement;*
> *For nothing can be sold or whole*
> *That has not been rent.*
> (William Butler Yeats, 1865-1939)

As it goes, I had not been born between piss and shit. I did not come through the typical door. No, I am no alien or test tube child. But, my mom had a C-section. The "C" stands for Cesarean. When I was young, I always thought the "C" was the shape of the incision the doctor would make. Cut a "C" and fold it open like a door for the baby to come out. Doctors don't cut C's but make an incision more like an "I" that splits open like a vagina. Maybe, they should call it an I-section as a procedure. Oh, no, wait, Cesarean doesn't start with "I."

Professor Locke continued his lecture. Moving the board with the crude drawing, he turned on a slide. The slide looked like this:

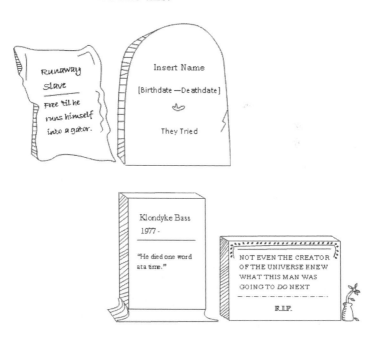

"If we are not cremated or evaporated by a nuclear weapon, the end of our life will be marked with one of these," he professed.

"It is the space between this point," he gestured to the crude drawing, "and this point" gesturing with the other hand to the tombstones, "that we must answer one question for ourselves."

He went back to the whiteboard and wrote the following sentence:

What is the Purpose of Life?

"Philosophy," he noted,"works to try to answer this question as well as others."

Dr. Locke was getting quite worked up. I could tell that he was passionate about his subject area.

"We will return to the question on the board throughout the semester, but I wish to begin by talking about ways of thinking," he said.

He went on to tell us that there were *only* two types of people. One type saw the world in black and white. They only had two categories for making judgments. He seemed to feel sorry for them. The other people, he went on, looked at an array of possible judgments. They, according to him, were philosophers.

Now, I was confused. He is a professor of philosophy, so I had assumed he was in the second category that he made. But, since he only made two categories, I felt that I was supposed to feel sorry for him.

...

Blossom walked into the philosophy class late. She had missed the opening discussions by Dr. Locke, but she looked as beautiful as ever. Upon entering, Blossom took the nearest seat to the door as to not disrupt the class. That seat was the furthest possible from where I sat. I craned my neck to try to get glimpses of her, but it was, for the most part, fruitless. What are the chances that I take only three classes and she is in all of them? It had to be destiny. I had to catch her after the class and talk to her.

...

Dr. Timothy Locke began discussing symbols that have philosophical depth. He started by explicating the various aspects of the Yin and Yang symbol. The symbol looked like this:

He talked about Taoism, balance or harmony, and lack of absolute purity of either side within the symbol. The dark had some light within it. The light had some dark.

After his quick explication of the Taoist symbol, he shifted to another.

"The Ouroboros is an ancient symbol," he stated.

The Ouroboros looked like a snake that had tied itself into a knot. Dr. Locke clicked a slide, and we saw the symbol for ourselves. It looked like this:

"It is," Locke went on, "a snake eating its tail. A symbol of infinity in which the snake cannot completely destroy itself."

He continued, "At best, the snake can eat itself into a smaller and smaller circle representing infinity, but it can never destroy the infinity that it depicts."

I raised my hand. Professor Locke was so focused on his diatribe regarding the snake eating itself that he did not at first notice me.

"Yes?"

"So, its only meaning is to try to destroy itself without the possibility of ever accomplishing that act," I asked.

"Isn't that plenty of meaning," he responded, curious where my question had stemmed from.

"Well," I said hesitantly, "I think there are other things going on."

"Really?" he questioned challengingly.

I did not like to be challenged. At times, I could even respond with an aggressive tone. I steadied myself.

"According to Plato's Timaeus, the snake's waste is providing him his own food. It is the nature of the symbol that it does not get smaller because having digested part of itself, it merely shits into its own mouth, providing nutrients to build the very piece it has eaten."

I paused. Gathering my thoughts, I realized I should have used the more proper word excrement rather than shit when talking to a professor.

"Rather than highlight the destructive nature of the snake as it tries to devour itself," I continued, "we can change the direction of our looking. On a circle, we can go both clockwise and counterclockwise. If we change the direction of our looking, the image appears to be a snake that is vomiting itself into existence. So, the infinity of the symbol can be a snake eating, shitting, or vomiting itself into or out of existence. At least the vomiting interpretation allows us to see it as producing something rather than eating crap or destroying something."

Dr. Locke seemed stunned.

"Right you are," he said, then added, "I was going to say just that." It was lie. Like you, I hate being lied to.

"You are quite an engaged student," he said to me, "You will make a fine Harvard alum someday, I'm sure." Little did he know.

...

I daydreamed for a moment that I could be a Harvard alum. There I was at my graduation ceremony in my silly gown and flat hat. The little hat was called a mortarboard. The individual presiding over the ceremony would say, "I now confer your applicable degree on you." And I, I would throw my mortarboard in the air haplessly. It would look like this:

It was a just a dream. I would never earn a college degree. Though, in another life, I would become a college professor.

•••

The Ouroboros has no beginning and no end. It is quite similar to the Tralfamadorians' response to Billy Pilgrim regarding time. There is just the amber of the moment. Thus, it may seem like Vonnegut sent his thoughts to the Faxer who sent them to me to send back to the Faxer, but it could very well be a different order. Maybe, I had the thoughts, wrote them, when the Faxer read them, the Faxer decided to freeze them in thought bubbles to send to the past where Vonnegut retrieved them from the TT machine. Time was messy.

•••

Listen:

I had finished Bass's book, *Gorge and Go Green*, about the ciao cow and decided to read something different. Before philosophy class started, I was halfway through Richard Wiseman's, *Quirkology: How we Discover Big Truth in Small Things*. Wiseman noted that research had found a significant relationship between a person's last name and his or her profession. For example, there were a disproportionate number of marine biologists named Dr. Fish. I chuckled as I thought of the Harvard professor's names. Lovejoy and psychology, Twane and literary theory, and Locke and philosophy appeared utterly cliché to me now.

...

The philosophy class ended, and I did my best to navigate the crowd to catch the lovely Blossom. She had just walked into the hall, but I was still trying to get around a small group of students who had congregated near the door. To be honest, I think I could have caught her if I had tried my best. But, I was still quite nervous about meeting her. She was stunning in everyway, and I doubted she would be interested in me. I found a way to not make into the hallway in time to get her attention. Had I known that she had waited outside after the literary theory class to thank me, I would have gone through hell to get to that hallway. As it was, I was not sure if our paths would ever cross again. But, I hoped for it.

SEVEN

Roland woke peacefully. He didn't have a defunct, Chinese alarm clock from the thrift shop. He had an expensive alarm clock that gradually increased its message over time until he woke. It also was embedded with AI or artificial intelligence. The clock "learned" from its user their waking patterns. Its rate and volume would adjust over time to best serve the sleeper in waking in a peaceful way. Knowing he had a lot to accomplish for the day, Roland got out of bed.

...

I woke from a nightmare in which a midget serial killer dressed as a panda bear was chasing me. My ill-programmed alarm clock never went off. I l ooked at it. The time displayed that it would begin spelling y-o-u in ten minutes. I switch off the alarm, so I would not have to listen to its repetitive error and got out of bed. I had a long day ahead.

...

Roland headed to his mancave. Sitting at his desk, he switched on the computer to double check his itinerary for the day. As the computer booted up, he picked up the postcard that sat on top of a stack of books on the right edge of his desk. The image on the card looked like this:

It was a flag of Bermuda. Roland had purchased a vacation package to head there later in the year. From Bermuda, he would travel to the Galapagos Islands. He wanted to see the fateful place that brought forth the thoughts of Darwin regarding evolution. Roland was sure that when he got there, he would understand why the Creator of the Universe had selected to make Whites the most advanced humans. He was sure the answer would be that Whites were ordained to eradicate non-Whites, but he was unsure how that message would get to him.

As Roland was about to place the postcard back where he had found it, he noticed the book that it sat on top of. Like the other books that were about crime and criminals, the top book was about Dennis Rader. Rader was better known as the BTK killer. BTK stood for bind, torture, and kill, which was Rader's MO or modus operandi. You may say that serial killers liked acronyms, but they didn't. They just liked to hurt, maim, and kill. BTK was the exception. He wrote letters signed BTK. Maybe, he thought he was in the business of killing and needed an acronym.

The BTK serial killer had a wife, but she never knew he was killing. It was easy to commit crimes for Roland because he had no one who would suspect anything. No wife, no family, nothing. Roland would make the BTK killer look like a stuffed panda bear bought at the zoo for a souvenir. BTK was caught,

Roland got away with his acts. Rader had a pattern, Roland did not.

In fact, the only error Roland would ever commit during his blue collar crime spree would be to read a piece of paper. What he read and what he didn't read would determine his fate.

...

I walked across the hardwood floor of my bedroom. My one bedroom condo was messy. I stubbed my left big toe on a box. Boxes were all over. I hadn't had time to unpack since my recent move to the condo. I was not wealthy, but I was comfortable. The investments I made in the youth of my career were paying off. I had bought the condo on a short sale. It was paid in full, which saved me the interest on a loan. In fact, the only debt I had was my student loans. I had nothing to show for all the money I borrowed to go to college, but I paid them monthly. They had a low enough interest rate that there was no need to rush into paying them. I would walk to work and had no car. A car would have just been another bill given its monthly loan payment, insurance, maintenance, etc. Etc. meant "et cetera," which was Latin for "and other things." It looked like this when written large:

I took a shower and got dressed for the day. My first obligation was to attend a rally. The rally was organized by a group to make people more aware of a case before the Supreme Court. The case focused on equal treatment for homosexuals. I had been invited by Dan Ogletree to it. Dan was my co-worker. He was gay. Out of the closet for more than ten years, Dan didn't look gay, he looked pretty much like all the other guys in my office.

Dan called and was outside waiting. He was picking me up in his car. We still had to drive to Ilium to attend the rally. Today was the first day of the three-day rally. I told Dan I would go with him on the first two days, but I had obligations for the third.

...

Roland left the Bermuda postcard on the stack of books and walked over to the costume and cosmetics area of his mancave. He was going to take on the attributes of Jeb Thompson. Jeb was one of the many identities he had paid to have constructed and was a 28 year old construction worker from Summersville, Tennessee.

Months back, Roland realized that the various false identities that he had created would drive vehicles different from the BMW, Mercedes, Jaguar, Aston Martin, Ferrari, Lamborghini, and Lotus that he owned. Roland had already sold the VW Beetle that he used to be subtle on the night he tortured and tattooed an unsuspecting gay man. About a month ago, he purchased a few inconspicuous cars to use in his exploits. A white, Ford F150 truck that was a couple years old and had a dent on the tailgate was purchased. Roland had it simultaneously registered to Jeb and Jenna Thompson of Summerville, Tennessee as well as

98

Tyler Greene of Dallas, Texas. He had plates for both TN and TX and would switch them depending on which false identity he was using. Such a ploy, Roland thought, may buy him time if the cops ever looked for him. They may pull over Jenna from TX while looking for Tyler from TN. It would give him a heads up that they were on to him. Similarly, he had bought a red, Honda civic that was about four years old, a grey, Chevy Traverse that was a year old, and a yellow, Chevy Camaro that was a couple years old. Each vehicle was registered under multiple names in multiple states. Roland had memorized which vehicle each personality he took on drove.

Roland put in his fake crooked and yellowed teeth. They were as crooked as a politician in Louisiana. After adding colored contacts to his ensemble, Roland went to one of the walk- in closets to get his attire. He put on a white t-shirt, some dusty jeans, and a flannel shirt. Placing a camouflage baseball cap that said Winchester on his head, he looked in the mirror to see if he looked the part of Jeb Thompson.

Roland's transformation into Jeb Thompson was nearly done. To complete the evolution, he needed to do a couple things. First, he went to the other room of the mancave. Roland switched the voice modulator from the broach he had wore when playing the role of Katie Holiday, who had hired Tank Rizo to kidnap and rape a senator, and placed it into generic dog tags. He set the modulator to deepen his voice but make no other changes to it. Roland tossed the dog tags over his head and tucked them under the white t-shirt. Second, he went back to the costume section of the mancave. Roland opened a drawer labeled "Jeb Thompson" and took out three items. One was a wallet with all the necessary fake IDs, including driver's license, insurance card, union member card, and credit cards. The other item was a can of dip. Dip is what people call chewing tobacco. Roland didn't use tobacco products, but he knew he had to give his various identities the habits of normal people. The third object was the key to the Ford F150. The key, with other generic keys to make it appear real, sat on a keychain that had the Confederate flag with the text "The South Will Rise Again."

Roland, as Jeb, headed to his garage to get the F150. He placed the Tennessee plates on the front and back of the truck. Roland jumped in and headed to downtown Ilium and the rally.

...

After leaving my condo, I headed down the staircase. I took one flight and was hit by a thought bubble. I had to get this out of me. It was like a disease. I could only be cured by vomiting all the words to the page. Sometimes, they came in chunks. Other times, there was a dry heaving that hurt and made me long for the nightmare to end. The thought bubble felt like super flu, while being electrocuted, while have lighter fluid poured on me and lit on fire. It was horrible.

I stumbled back up the steps and got to my home. Shaking, I headed to my computer. Having experienced this too often, I now had a habit of leaving the computer running.

Feeling like I was burning up inside, I began to type. The words flew from my mind through my fingers onto the page. The first words were:

100

The Voyager made three more stops over the next six hours.

After fifteen minutes of nonstop typing, my cellphone rang. I was sure it was Dan, who was getting impatient. As it rang, I knew I would have to come up with an excuse, but I couldn't answer it. I had to get these words out. Five minutes later, the thought bubble had passed. I had written multiple pages.

I left and met Dan at his car downstairs.

His look asked, "What took so long?"

"Sorry, big dump," I answered.

It was not a lie. I dumped words to page rather than shit to a toilet.

We took off and head to Ilium.

...

Roland parked a couple blocks from the downtown area of Ilium where the rally was being held. He locked the truck and put some dip in his lower lip. Roland had never dipped, and his eyes watered from the intense burn in his mouth. Saliva was building fast in his mouth to cool the burn. He didn't know how often he should spit. He spit. Brown colored saliva hit the bright grey sidewalk. This isn't so bad, he thought, as he wiped a tear from his cheek.

After walking the two blocks to the downtown area, Roland knew he was close. He could hear the chats of numerous individuals. Roland couldn't understand what they were saying because two groups were in a shouting match. He turned the corner and saw a large group of white guys. Across the street was a larger group. It was mixed with women, blacks, Asians, Hispanics, and all sorts of other people. Most were probably gay, he thought. He knew which group to go to.

As Roland got close the homogeneous group, a tall, bearded lumberjack character holding a sign that said "Faggots don't nede rights. They nede therapee," turned and addressed him.

"Who are you?"

"Roland...," he paused and thought, "in the hay"

"Huh," the lumberjack said dumbfounded.

"Didn't you ask me where I done come from?" Roland said with a Southern draw.

"No, I said, Who are you?"

"Oh, Jeb...Jeb Thompson," he nudged the guy, "I just come from a roll'n the hay with a cute, little Southern belle. Still got'r on my mind"

Roland didn't think his identity was compromised. He had recovered fairly quickly, and the lumberjack didn't seem all that bright. He had spelled almost half the words on his sign incorrectly.

...

Dan parked the car and grabbed his sign from the back of his car. It read, "We hold these truths to be self-evident, that all people are created equal." Dan had changed the word "man" in the original expression to encompass women and had underlined the word "equal."

We walked to the rally. Dan knew a few of the individuals there. I didn't know anyone there but Dan. Dan was enveloped by the large group, and I lost sight of him. I decided to head to the front of the group, near the road, to see the adjacent group on the other side of the street.

The other group was composed entirely of White males. Their signs were full of hate and distrust. Did they have any friends who were not White? Weren't any of their friends gay? I thought. I doubted it.

A tall dark-skinned male with a hideous scar on his neck stood next to me. His sign said, "I will not yield to your hate." He looked at me and started a conversation.

"Nice of you to join us."

"Thanks, I came with my friend Dan," I said.

"I'm Juan Jackson, but people call me JJ," he said extending his hand.

I told him my name as I shook his outstretched hand.

Talking, I found out that Juan's father was Black, his mother was Mexican, and he was gay. He noticed that my eyes would wander to his neck and the large scar. I couldn't help looking at it. What caused it? I wondered. I had never seen such a scar.

"You're looking at my scar," JJ said laughing.

"Uh, well, yeah, sorry," I stumbled to say.

"It's okay, it draws attention."

I was unsure what I was supposed to say in response.

"How about you and me go get some coffee, and I'll tell you the story about it," JJ asked. JJ wanted some coffee to give him a boost. He had been at the rally for a few hours and had skipped breakfast. When near such hate groups, he never liked leaving the pack without, at least, one other person.

I wanted to know about the scar, but I was unsure if JJ was asking me on a date or just being friendly. Female friends of mine had told me of such confusing moments when a man asked them to such a meeting, but I had never experienced it firsthand. My hesitation must have been noted by JJ.

"I'm not looking for a date," he said, "I have a boyfriend."

JJ had said it in such a way as to put me at ease.

"Okay," I replied, "there's a coffee shop just around the corner." I had seen it as Dan and I were walking from the car.

...

Roland was enjoying impersonating a redneck from Tennessee. Jeb became a fairly flamboyant figure in the all White male group. He would tell others how much he'd like to just string up some of those niggers, faggots, and spicks. Most in the group agreed, but a minority were offended by his suggestions of violence. Roland got a rush knowing that there were others who had neo-Nazi tendencies.

He realized that his persona was becoming a distraction to his mission. Jeb was not there to become popular with the crowd. He was there to do some recon. The three day rally had drawn together his enemies, and he needed to select his next targets. Being the first day, his goal was to select two people to kill. He planned for one to be killed tomorrow. The other, he would kill on the last day of the rally.

...

JJ and I headed to the little coffee shop around the corner. On our way, JJ told me he was a public defender of a nearby city. Defending the weak from the strong was in his blood, and he loved his job. Later, I would see him on TV.

We carried on small talk as we waited for our coffee. After finding a small table near the entrance, JJ went on to tell me that a few years back two men had jumped a gay friend of his who had left the local gay bar, the Clair De Lune. JJ had been at the club, too. JJ's friend had told JJ he was leaving, and JJ had forgotten to tell his friend something. JJ left the club to track down his friend only to find his friend being severely beaten by two men. Rushing to his friend's defense, he had tackled one of the assailants. The second assailant came to *his* friend's aid. JJ was stuck in the head by a blunt object that he never saw coming. He didn't know what it was, but it "hurt like hell" according to him. Barely conscious, JJ lay by his friend believing the worse had passed.

One of the assailants stood guard over the two helpless gay men. The other ran to get their truck. JJ could hear a vehicle coming down the alley, but he had no strength to get up. The truck stopped. The two gay-bashers took a rope from the back of the truck, made a noose, and hung it over JJ's head. They had tied the other end of the rope to the truck's roll bars. A minute later JJ was being dragged down the alley by his neck. After three blocks, the truck was stopped by police who had been called by someone who saw the events unfolding. JJ lived, but he carried a scar from the rope burn of that fateful night.

"Can it be removed?" I asked.

"Why would I want it to be?" he responded, "it's a constant reminder of who I am and where I have been."

"Really?" I questioned, unsure of why anyone would keep such a hideous scar.

"Yeah," JJ asserted, "and I still go about twice a month to visit the two guys in prison."

"Really?" I said astounded.

"Violence only leads to more violence. Hate only to hate. It is through love that hate is conquered," he claimed.

He continued, "Those two poor souls are merely sand missing their pebble."

"Huh," I exhaled confused.

"Do you know where we get a circle for the number zero?" he asked. The number zero was a circle that looked like this:

$$O$$

"Uh, what does a zero have to do with any of this? Or pebbles and sand?" I inquired.

"The number zero comes from an old Indian counting system where they used pebbles as numbers. The pebbles lay in the sand for the Indians to do their math. If a pebble was removed, it left a divot. The divot was the absence of a number and was the circular form of the missing pebble." JJ lectured.

"So?" I said hoping that he would connect that pieces that my mind could not.

"Humans desire love. It is a basic need. We are the sand and the love of another fills our gap or incompleteness. Without a pebble, we feel empty and hate grows. Those two poor boys were full of hate because they lacked a pebble."

I almost laughed.

"So," I said, "you think visiting them in prison is a way to provide them with the pebble that they are missing."

"I don't know," said JJ, "but forgiveness, acceptance, and respect are powerful things."

After only a twenty minute cup of coffee with the man, I felt as if I had known JJ for many years. We left and headed back to the rally.

•••

Dressed as Jeb, Roland made his way through the White male crowd to the front near the street. What a horrid bunch of characters, he thought, as he looked across the street. Jeb scanned the crowd looking for his targets. He had a hard time picking. In his mind, all of them should be eradicated. They were a plague on society, and he was the antidote.

Jeb fantasized about killing every one of them, right here, right now. In his imagination, he had a Gatling gun on a small tripod. Organizing in the center of the all White male group, Jeb would ready the weapon. "Now", he yelled, and the others in his group parted. He cranked the Gatling gun and mowed down the other group in droves. They would be helpless to run or fight. He had all the power.

Roland shook his head and came out of his daydream with a smile on his face.

•••

On the way back to the rally, JJ and I met a young entrepreneur. She had set up a small table about a half a block from the rally and was selling t-shirts, signs, and buttons with political slogans on them.

In her jeans, baggy t-shirt, sunglasses, and baseball cap, I hardly recognized her. It was Blossom. I had to meet her now.

"Hold up," I told JJ, "I want to look over this stuff." I stopped at the table.

Walking over to the table, Blossom recognized me.

"Aren't you a student at Harvard?" she inquired.

I started to lie. Like you, I don't like being lied to. So, I decided against it.

"Uh, no, I was just visiting classes there for a while."

Thinking I had meant that I had dropped out of Harvard, she laughed playfully.

"Well, school isn't for everyone."

"Oh, I know, boy, do I know."

"I wanted to thank you for interrupting Dr. Twane's interrogation of me."

I felt nervous. She really did remember me.

"It was nothing," I said bashfully.

Not wanting to seem as if I liked her too much, I tried to shift into the cold, factual tone of business.

"How much for the t-shirt?" I asked.

"One for 15 or two for 20," she responded. She had been asked that question numerous times over the half hour that she had set up shop, so her response was almost automated.

Most of the shirts had sayings that labeled the wearer as gay. "I'm gay, get over it" and "I'll stop

108

being gay, when you stop being straight" were the two most common in the stack. I did, however, find one that seemed to fit my position in all this and send the message to Blossom that I was not gay. The black t-shirt had a large, red heart at its center. Above the heart was the word "Hetero ally" and below was "equality."

I selected the shirt and paid Blossom. Our eyes met for a long instant, and I knew she was my pebble. She gave me back my change.

I wanted to ask her out, then and there, but I could not get the words out. Instead, I put the shirt on to show her that it was for me.

"Fits good," I said dumbly.

"Yeah, I'm glad you are supporting the right side."

Oh, no, I thought, is she a lesbian? Have I lost my chance?

"I am too," she continued smiling. Blossom held out her bracelet that had the same saying as the shirt I was now wearing. The train tracks of our individual lives were meeting each other.

"Good," I said. Really? Really? The best thing you thought of was to say good, I berated myself.

Another customer came and asked about the shirts. The moment had faded.

I turned to walk away. Blossom held up a single finger to the new customer noting that she would help them in one minute.

"By the way, I'm Blossom," she said, as my back was now to her.

I turned around, told her my name, shook her hand, and told her that it was nice to meet her finally.

"Would you like to go out sometime?" I said before I lost my nerve again.

"Sure," she said with a smile that put me at ease.

With her school obligations and my various commitments, we realized that our first date would be delayed for quite some time. It didn't matter. I was elated that I would have a date with this remarkable woman. My spirit soared.

JJ and I headed back to the rally. I had a spring in my step. JJ looked at me and smiled.

"See, that, that is the impact of a pebble on a person," he said. I could tell he was happy for me.

...

Roland stood at the front of his pack. Scanning the other crowd, he could not think of which two should be his victims. They all seem like good candidates, he thought.

He paused. There, there near the center of the front were the two that needed to die, he thought. Roland saw a tall, well-dressed, dark-skinned man holding a sign. His sign appeared to be a challenge to Roland. "I will not yield to your hate," Roland mumbled to himself. No, you will die before my power, he thought.

Roland could feel the anger growing within him. He could not believe the audacity of the guy next to the sign holder. The guy is the worst of the worst, Roland thought, and a traitor to the cause. Roland was staring at a male wearing a black t-shirt that said "Hetero ally" heart "equality."

Roland despised, with the deepest of hate, traitors. He was sure it was why Dante made clear that

110

the lowest level of hell consisted of only Judas Iscariot, Brutus, and Cassius. Roland was certain that the gay-loving traitor would be his next victim. There was no place in the world for such a traitor, and he would make sure that there was one less of those despicable roaches crawling around.

...

Standing next to JJ, I shouted the equality chants of the crowd and gazed at the group across the street. After my talk with JJ, I somewhat felt sorry for them. They were hurting and hateful because they had no pebble.

One member of the group across the street stood out. He was dressed similar to others with jeans, a white t-shirt, and a flannel. He was wearing a Winchester cap that was camouflage. Although he looked like a clone of the average protester in that crowd, he was staring at me. His eyes seemed full of excitement and malicious with harmful intent. I shuttered.

EIGHT

The TT technicians took the halo off of Vonnegut's head. He felt exhausted, as if he had gone without sleep for a day or so. Vonnegut could barely keep his eyes open.

"Are we finished?" Vonnegut asked the white lab coat.

"No," the technician responded, "it's just lunch time."

The technician finished unhooking Vonnegut from the TT machine, and a guard came to escort him to the cafeteria.

...

Dr. Darnell Durling Heath sat at his desk reading the newest issue of his Ghost Shirt Society newsletter. He set down the newsletter and picked up a small orange sphere. It was one of the many thought bubbles collected. Within the sphere, the thoughts of the woman who would tell Judy and Hilda of Merriam's death, Karen Von Gleiss, had been stored. At least, some of them. Hieroglyphic-like symbols, strange and seemingly alive, moved within the semitransparent ball. Heath examined them, but he had no idea what they meant.

An aide entered. Heath set the thought bubble down.

"Sir," the aide began, "the first stage for all participants is now complete."

The aide was carrying a box filled with Vonnegut's thought bubbles and set it on the edge of Heath's desk.

"The C group of participants are now at the cafeteria getting lunch," he reported, "and they were the last group to need lunch."

"Okay," Heath had responded as his administrative assistant stepped in the doorway.

"Can I have a moment?" the administrative assistant said to Heath.

"Sure."

Heath got up from his chair and walked around his desk.

"By the way," the aide said as Heath walked passed to meet with his administrative assistant, "you might want to get some lunch too."

"I will," Heath mumbled, "just get the thought bubbles to the storage system."

The aide picked up the box of Vonnegut's bubbles. How did that one fall out? He thought. The aide grabbed the random, orange bubble that was sitting on Heath's desk and added it to the box of Vonnegut's thoughts.

...

I had left the rally, and Dan had driven me straight to work. My supervisor gave me a disapproving look when he noticed my t-shirt. I had forgotten that I had put it on. Raising my hands as if surrendering, I pulled the black t-shirt off. The supervisor nodded his approval.

Entering my small office, I turned my computer on and set my phone to accept calls. A friendly co-worker came in to ask if I had gotten the last memo that was sent to all Customer Service Representative or CSRs.

As I started to tell her that I had just got into the office, a thought bubble overtook me. I stuttered, "I…I…I…I…jussssss…."

She must have thought I was having a stroke or a seizure. The co-worker rushed to my side.

"You okay?" she kept asking.

"I'll be fine," I fought the bubble to say to her, "just let me work"

"But…" she began.

I interrupted, "You can come check on me in 30 minutes or so."

She was uncertain whether she should leave me. The bubble was growing in my mind. I would not be able to fight it much longer to talk to her. I had to write now.

"Please," I begged.

"Ok," she said, "but I will be *right* back."

The computer was on. I opened the word processing application and typed. The first words hit the page:

Bass had written a number of books and short stories.

I typed nonstop for 20 minutes. The thoughts faded.

My co-worker came back in.

"Everything alright?" she asked.

"Yeah," I said, "I feel much better now."

"You should go to a doctor. That was strange," she asserted.

It was strange. I needed to see a doctor. Why it never occurred to me was because I thought it was a temporary issue. But, what if it wasn't? Tomorrow, I was going to the rally in the morning and work in the afternoon. The following day was the beginning of my vacation, so I called the doctor and set an appointment for tomorrow late in the day.

...

Escorted by a guard, Vonnegut entered the large cafeteria of the TT facility. His left ear was humming and ached. He didn't know why. Maybe, it was just old age, he thought. He went through the line and got beef pot roast, mash potatoes, corn, and green beans. Vonnegut took his tray to a table and sat it down. He walked over to the drink station and got a cup of ice and filled it with sugarless tea. The Great Author of the 20th Century walked back to his table.

As he headed back, he noticed that a middle age women with coal black hair was sitting across from his tray of food.

"Mr. Vonnegut?," she said smitten, as he approached.

"Yes," he responded.

"Karen Von Gleiss," she announced, with a lovely smile, "I'm a big fan."

Karen had only read Slaughterhouse Five. She enjoyed the war message within its pages. Von Gleiss didn't read often and was worried that the next book would be a waste of time. A future book may not be as good as one you already read. Karen read Slaughterhouse Five about every three months. It was one of only five books that she continuously read.

"Really?," said Vonnegut, "it's always nice to meet a fan."

116

Vonnegut rubbed his left ear. There was pressure in it and humming and an annoying ache. The rubbing didn't help.

"You are so great," Karen proclaimed to Vonnegut, "I think you ought to be President of the United States!" Her words rang out as if in cursive, fluidly without the rigidity of block print. If one could have seen those words, they would have looked like this:

You ought to be President of the United States!

"I don't really know about that," Vonnegut responded, "but thank you."

Vonnegut took a bite of his pot roast and shoved a scoop of green beans in his mouth. The pot roast tasted like dried cow dung smothered with week old gravy. He wished he would have gotten the hamburger instead. A hamburger looks like this:

Karen was a chatterbox. She talked to Vonnegut about her job, her friends Judy and Hilda, her love life, her recent trip to the doctor, her dog, her college days, her favorite recipe, and her love of Bach. Vonnegut listened quietly and patiently.

"By the way," she went on, "a participant named Merriam Beauveax died yesterday, here."

Vonnegut became more attentive.

"Really?" he asked. He was unaware that it was the same lady whose perfume almost gagged him in the van on the way to the project.

"I'm not sure what happened," Karen stated, "but I'm sure she's dead."

Leaning forward and speaking in almost a whisper, Karen asked, "do you think they killed her?"

Vonnegut shook his head.

"I don't think they have any reason to harm any of us," he said, "we're their lab rats."

Having finished much of the grotesque food on his tray, Vonnegut was approached by a guard.

"124C?" the guard asked.

"Yes," Vonnegut responded.

"It's time to finish your allotted time with the technicians."

"Okay, you lead the way," he said.

Vonnegut headed to participate in the second and final stage of the TT project.

NINE

Blossom was slow dancing with me. Our bodies close, my mind racing, and my desire expanding. The slow love song was coming to an end. She looked up at me and smiled. I leaned in and gave her a tender kiss. Blossom responded with a more passionate one.

"Let's go back to my place," she whispered in my ear.

I was excited. I couldn't reply.

She whispered more, "All I want is you, y-o-u, y-o-u, y-o-u, y-o-u…"

My alarm clock was going off.

I awoke with a longing to return to the dream.

...

Roland worked quickly to extract the poison, ricin, from the castor beans he had ordered. Oh, I cannot wait to kill that traitor today, he kept thinking to himself. He continued in his thought, by the end of today, that traitor will be in the company of Judas, Brutus, and Cassius, the most horrid level of hell.

Roland had learned of the deadly toxin ricin while reading about the assassinations of various figures. Bulgarian dissident, Georgi Markov, had been killed with an umbrella. Umbrellas were usually harmless. The assassin, however, had placed ricin on the tip of the umbrella and had merely poked his prey. With no cure, Markov died four days later. The stuff was potent, as little as 500 micrograms, about the size of a pinhead, would likely kill an adult.

Instead of an umbrella, Roland had employed a local, engineering student to construct a crutch with a needle spring loaded on its bottom. A switch on the handle would push the needle out. The needle and spring were designed to pierce through even steel toed boots. Roland was going to accidentally set the leg of the crutch on his prey's foot and hit the switch. He would kill them with what would appear the accident of a cripple. Roland smiled thinking about it.

•••

I got up and started to get ready for the day. It was going to be a busy day. I had the rally to attend, work, and a doctor's appointment.

•••

Roland got dressed as Tyler Greene, a small business owner from Dallas, Texas. He put on a cheap suit and dress shoes. The shoes were designed to subtly make him appear two inches taller. He needed to match the height listed on Greene's driver's license. Roland placed the fake, blonde goatee on his face and the matching blonde wig on his head. He pulled the lengthy hair into a ponytail. He placed an open pack of Pall Malls and a lighter in his shirt pocket. Roland decided to forgo the usual tie he wore when he was Tyler in order to appear more casual.

The fake cast that would nearly complete his transformation was in the other area of the mancave. Roland browsed the numerous casts piled up in the corner. He selected one with no writing on it. For the next twenty minutes, Roland filled the cast with fake signatures, quotes, and images. He was going to play a gay male in this scene of his life, so he made certain to color a number of rainbows and equal signs on the white plaster. "When this comes off," one of his writings stated, "let's go dancing at the gay club again – John W." Roland made sure to vary his writing as much as possible and used some stencils with cursive writing from time to time. He didn't want this cast to be his undoing.

With the cast decorated and placed on his left, lower leg, Roland looked for the special crutch he had had constructed. He had two built, but he planned on taking only one. Better test it, he thought. The first crutch had a trigger mechanism that was too sensitive for Roland's taste. He tested the other. It worked to his liking. He practiced walking with the crutch to make sure that it appeared he had done so for a while. Roland didn't realize that he was doing it incorrectly. The cast was on his left leg, so he put the crutch on that side to act as an extra leg. Fact was, doctors told patients to use crutches on the opposite side of the injury because people overestimate the value of the crutch and end up putting too much pressure on the injured leg. Roland thought he had it down, but any other individual watching would have told him he looked silly and fake.

Roland went back to his desk and grabbed two, pea-sized spheres. Each was filled with ricin. The ricin was contained in a fragile, plastic ball. He took one and carefully placed it in the socket of the crutch. When he was ready to kill, he would click the hidden trigger, the spring would release, and the needle would pierce the ball and be covered in ricin. There was a hundred times more ricin in each ball than was needed, but Roland would rather overdo it. He put the other sphere in his pant pocket just in case there was a misfire and he needed to reload the crutch.

Walking over to the costume area of the mancave, Roland opened a drawer labeled "Tyler Greene." He took the necessary accessories out and headed to the garage.

After switching the F150's plates from Tennessee to Texas, Roland left and headed to the rally.

...

Dan called.

"Are you ready?" he asked.

"I'll be down in a sec," I replied.

I grabbed a small, pocket notepad and pen and headed out the door. With the number of thought bubbles that were bombarding me lately, I had gotten in the habit of having something to write with. One can never be too careful. Later, I would go to the doctor and explain this bizarre phenomenon. I was anxious about the appointment, but I was hopeful that she would find something to cure me.

I got to the car and sat down in the passenger seat.

"That was fast," Dan said, "are you sure you're ready? Don't need to take a monster dump do you?"

He continued, "I mean, I could wait. It's not like I haven't before."

Embarrassed by his teasing, I responded, "No, no, I'm good, let's just go."

Dan and I headed to Ilium and the rally for its second day.

...

Roland parked the truck, walked passed a coffee shop, and headed to the enemies' lair. He tried to

122

mentally prepare himself. Gays would be all around him. He vowed to use the ricin on any of them who pinched his ass or touch him in any way that was sexual.

The crowd had grown exponentially from the previous day. It was so large of a gathering on both sides of the street that it took up more than one block. People were coming to rally from near and far. Almost all fifty states were represented on the side that Roland was heading to. The other side of the street lacked such demographic representation. They were missing a representative from Alaska, Hawaii, California, Oregon, Washington, Colorado, Nevada, North Dakota, Massachusetts, Rhode Island, and Florida. Such large crowds also drew the media. News vans lined the street. Cameras were everywhere.

Roland should have been nervous to execute his plan with all the cameras around, but he was so focused on his hate and the pure joy he got from doing blue collar crime that he didn't even reflect on the potential hazard that cameras would bring to the situation. Between my disguise, fake injury, and sunglasses, I'm as safe here as anywhere, he thought. He entered the mass of people, wobbling on his fake broke leg and crutch, looking for the traitor. Roland knew he was there. It was Roland's destiny to kill him, and he was going to do anything necessary to see that destiny fulfilled.

...

Dan and I parked. It was further from the rally compared to yesterday because of all the additional vehicles the rally had drawn to it, but it was roughly in the same area. We headed toward the rally. I knew we would pass the coffee shop and, potentially, the little table that Blossom had set up yesterday. I was anxious to see her again and hoped she was there.

As we turned the corner near the coffee shop, I saw a blonde man with a ponytail in a business suit struggling along with one crutch. It seemed that he had broken his left leg. He appeared awkward with the crutch and was using it on the wrong side of his body. If I saw him in the crowd, I would have to make sure and tell him. He shouldn't be too hard to find in the crowd.

We walked further, and I found that Blossom's table was being run by someone else. I knew that she said she had to study for a test this week when we were trying to find a time to go on our first date. In fact, Blossom was at the library studying for her sociology exam.

I was wearing the shirt I had bought from her yesterday. Not only did it remind me of her but it was also the only thing I owned that made a political statement. I didn't care that I had just wore it yesterday. It seemed to fit the occasion.

Realizing that I could use some caffeine, I told Dan that I was heading back to the coffee shop, and I would find him in the crowd. Dan headed on, sign in hand, ready to demonstrate. Meanwhile, I went to the coffee shop and got an espresso.

"Make it a triple," I told the barista, "and no foam."

As I waiting for the coffee, I notice a painting on the wall. I did not see it yesterday because I was so caught up in my conversation with JJ. It was a man's

124

face with a single tear and, while simple, was quite moving. It looked like this:

Maybe the man was simply missing his pebble.

•••

Roland hobbled through the crowd, but he saw no sign of the traitor or the dark-skinned man that was next to the traitor yesterday. There were plenty of other targets, but Roland was committed to his task. Find the traitor and kill him.

A voice from the crowd interrupted his thoughts.

"Glad you could make it, with the injury and all," the voice repeated.

"Wouldn't miss this chance," Roland, as Tyler Greene, replied with a smile.

Roland realized that in his haste to leave he had forgotten the voice modulator. He would just have to limit how many people he talked to and try to ignore any who were nice enough to start a conversation.

...

I got to the rally but didn't see Dan anywhere. The crowd was large and dense. I headed toward the street-side of the group and ran into JJ.

"How are you?" he asked sincerely.

"I'm good, yourself?"

"Can't complain. I have an interview with one of the TV stations in a bit," he added.

"Nice"

"You should come with me. I'll introduce you to a couple of the reporters I know."

"Okay," I said without thinking.

We headed to the front of the edge of the street-side where all the news affiliates were.

"Hey, do you wanna be in the shot?" JJ asked.

"I don't know," I replied hesitantly.

"Man, I've been on TV before cause of big cases, but everyone should have a shot to be seen by the television audience," he added, "You're doing it, I won't take no for an answer."

"But…" I started.

JJ interrupted, "No buts, I told you that I won't take no for an answer."

•••

Roland located the traitor and the tall, dark-skinned male from yesterday. The traitor was still wearing the same t-shirt professing his treason. He was probably just a poor schmuck that found it easier to befriend these faggots, Roland thought.

With the crutch, he slowly moved through the crowd to try to get closer to his target.

•••

JJ checked that his tie was well adjusted and prepared to talk to the media. I stood to his left. The triple espresso was getting to me. I had to pee. The nearest bathroom was either the coffee shop or, in the other direction, the office supply store. I would wait. Hold it, I told myself, just hold it.

JJ introduced me to Lindsey Che, a reporter from an affiliate out of Philadelphia.

"Nice to meet you," I said.

"Nice to meet you, too."

Che went on, "Do you mind being in the shot? I think your shirt will make for good context next to Mr. Jackson." She wanted JJ for his scarred neck and backstory as well as his position as a public defender. Che only wanted me because of my shirt. I was a prop.

"You can call me JJ, for now" stated JJ, "and we can be more formal when the cameras are rolling."

"I don't mind being in the shot," I responded, wiggling somewhat because my need-to-piss-right-now feeling was growing. I was cursing the intern who had brought the wrong camera and was running to get the right one. Had he brought the right one, I might not end up pissing myself on live television. I tried to think of Blossom to get my mind off of it. It wasn't helping much.

I kept my feet moving. Someone watching my feet would probably think I had four left feet and was trying to learn the Texas two-step.

...

Roland had snuck up behind the two unsuspecting individuals. He could see that the news was about to interview one of those assholes. Which one got interviewed didn't matter to Roland, but the traitor was about to be poisoned.

The crowd was pushing Roland ever closer to the two. Everyone wanted to be in the camera frame, and Roland had the prime real estate. The traitor was on his right, and the tall dark-skinned male was on his left.

How am I going to do this? He thought. Roland would have to switch which side the crutch was on or find some other means for using the crutch to pierce the shoe of the traitor.

...

I had to go to the bathroom so bad that I was nearly in pain. My legs shuffled trying to buy me more time. My left elbow swung as I wiggled around and made solid contact with an individual behind me.

"Ouch," the voice cried out.

I turned and saw the man with the crutch.

"Oh, I am so, so sorry," I said.

"Listen," I began, "Mr., uhm, what's your name?"

"Greene, Tyler Greene," Roland said in huff. There was something eerily familiar about Tyler, but I couldn't place it. Before it was all over, I would not make the connection between the crooked teethed, Winchester cap wearing Jeb and Tyler.

"Mr. Greene, I would like to make it up to you. I saw a place to buy medical supplies like crutches when my friend and I were driving here. I'll get you another crutch, and it will be easier for you to get around." It was a dumb thing to say, but I couldn't think of anything else.

Distracted by the turn of events, Roland had temporarily forgotten his mission.

"So, it's *my* fault, *you* elbowed me?," he aggressively responded, "I don't need your damn help."

"Okay, okay," I said, as I felt JJ tap my shoulder.

"It's time," JJ stated matter-of-factly. JJ had seen the intern a half a block away.

The intern finally showed up and placed the correct camera on his shoulder. Che had her back to the street and was talking to JJ. Tapping Che on the shoulder, the intern gave her the thumbs up, so she would know that he was ready.

"Okay," Che said to JJ, "I'm going to have my back to you and face the camera to introduce the story, then, I will turn around and interview you."

"Are you okay?" Che asked me due to all my dancing around.

"I'm okay," I answered, "just want to get done with this."

Che turned to face the camera. The intern held up three fingers, then two, then one.

"Lindsey Che, here, reporting from the fine city of Ilium, New York," she began.

...

What the hell? Roland thought to himself, the traitor bastard had the gall to elbow me.

Roland moved in close. He thought those on camera would just think he was trying harder to get in the frame. It was great that they were distracted.

He lifted the crutch slightly off the ground and prepared to stumble and place it on the foot of the traitor. Clicking the trigger mechanism the ricin would be injected, and the traitor would be no more. Roland watched the feet of the traitor to time his act. Those feet were shifting and moving like mad. It was as if the traitor knew Roland's intentions.

Roland paused to think through his plan of action more. Given the shifty feet of the traitor, his position between his two prey, and the prominence the newswoman was giving to the dark-skinned male, he thought he should flip the order of his murders. I really want to kill the traitor, but this is a prime moment to take out the faggot, he thought. Maybe, Roland reflected, it would strike fear in the traitor and the last day of that cockroach's life will be lived in paranoia.

...

I could take it no longer. I had to piss. The interview with JJ was only just beginning, but I had fought my body as long as I possibly could. I turned quickly around to get out of the dense crowd.

In my haste, I bumped into Mr. Greene.

"Sorry, again," I said with great humility. I didn't stop. Either I was going to have my bladder burst and kill me with toxins in my body or I was going to piss myself in front of a large crowd. Neither seemed appealing. So, I moved rapidly like a man on a mission to get out of the crowd.

•••

Roland saw the traitor turn but could not get out of his way fast enough. The traitor looked as if he was in a panic and slammed into the right shoulder of Roland.

Roland used the moment to implement his plan. He lifted the crutch from the ground and accidentally fell forward and to his left. The crutch landed squarely on JJ's right shoe. Roland leaned on the crutch as if he needed it to regain his balance. The weight of Roland alone would have bruised JJ's foot.

Tyler Greene pulled the trigger, and a needle laced with liquid death penetrated JJ's foot.

•••

"Ow, fuck!" JJ exclaimed.

Che leaned closer, "We're live, you can't say that."

JJ turned and saw the man with the crutch.

"Sorry, I'm so sorry," the man said with a smirk on his face.

"It's okay," JJ said, "it's crowded, but be careful, you don't want to break someone else's toe."

After finding out about his injury, JJ would have prayed for a broken toe or two or ten.

JJ shook his head. The guy probably just wanted the media's attention, he thought.

"I'll be careful," the crutch wielding man said, "and get out of your way."

Roland disappeared into the crowd.

...

I was running in the direction of the coffee shop. It seemed closer than the office supply store that was in the opposite direction. Then, it hit me. A thought bubble burst into my psyche. I shook and stumbled. Damn it, not now!

I withdrew the miniature notebook and pen that I had remembered to bring with me when Dan called me earlier. The pen did not work. My own thoughts rushed to find a solution.

The ache from the bubble was so intense it took my thoughts from my need to urinate. Tears welled in my eyes from the pain of the thoughts. I rushed into the coffee shop and scanned the clientele. Two, different individuals were on their laptops. I moved quickly over to the closest one.

"I need to use your laptop," I said to the young man.

"Huh"

"I *need* to use your laptop," I repeated.

"No way, dude," he said.

I struggled to get my wallet out. My hands were shaking intensely and a sweat beaded on my forehead.

"I'll give you $20 bucks for ten minutes," I said. Opening my wallet, I realized I only had a one hundred dollar bill.

"Scratch that, I'll give you $100 bucks for ten minutes," I stated, showing him the bill.

"Uhm, okay," he said, as he took the cash.

I sat and opened an email to myself. The words came crashing out. It began:
They laughed stupidly like only fraternity brothers can.

My typing was nonstop and quick. After five minutes, it was all out.

...

JJ felt a burning sensation in his right foot. Man that guy really speared me with his crutch, he thought. Little did he know.

As the interview concluded and he could focus his attention on his pain, he realized that a warm liquid smothered his foot and was soaked up by his sock. It was his blood. He wouldn't know that until later when he took his shoes off at home.

He would be dead in 30 hours.

...

After sending the email of the words to myself, warm liquid drenched my pants and dripped by my foot. My bladder had had enough. With the thought bubble gone, my mind had no distraction. It could not wait any longer for me to find a place to discard my waste.

Embarrassed, I stood up.

"Dude, you just pissed yourself," the laptop owner announced.

"I know," I replied shaking my head.

Everyone was looking at me. I headed to the bathroom to try to figure out how to clean up.

"Man, didn't you already go?" asked the barista mockingly. I entered the bathroom with my head down in shame.

Unlike the bowels of Merriam's guard that had let her die, my bladder had saved me from certain death. It was too bad that it didn't save me from this ridicule.

TEN

Dan drove me home from the rally. Originally, he was going to drop me off at work, which wasn't far from my condo, but, with my urine-soaked pants, I had to go home and get cleaned up. Dan was kind enough not to mention or tease me about the incident. He knew that I had suffered enough since I had to go into the crowd of the rally to tell him I needed to go.

"Thanks, I appreciate it," I stated as I got out at my home.

"No problem, and thanks for coming to the rally with me in the first place," Dan noted.

"It's an important cause and needs people like you," he added.

I smiled back, but it wasn't much of a smile since I was mentally exhausted from the day's events. And I still have to go to work, and the doctor, I thought.

We said our goodbyes and made plans for when I came back from my upcoming vacation.

•••

Roland got back to his mansion and got out of his Tyler Greene costume. He found himself in a state of painful bliss. On the hand, he was so overjoyed that he had completed his mission. The dark-skinned man was going to die slowly from the poison Roland had injected into his foot. But, on the other hand, he had wanted so bad to kill that traitor. The traitor must die.

Tossing the blonde haired wig in the corner, Roland went over to his gun safe and entered the code. He had his new plan already in mind. Eleven guns filled the safe. Some were assault rifles, some shotguns, and some handguns. He took the .45 caliber revolver out and looked at it. It looked like this:

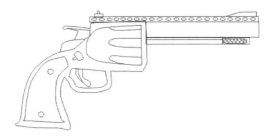

Roland had purchased some of the guns legally, but this one was special. He had bought it from a black market dealer. It had been used in so many felonies that if it were confiscated or lost it would trace to so many criminals as to be nearly useless. The gun had quite a history. It had been used in 29 murders, 38 attempted murders, 15 carjackings, and 82 armed robberies. The gun seemed destined for a life a crime. It had been confiscated and put in police evidence only once. The gun stayed in police custody for less than 24 hours. A bold, armed gang had raided the evidence room that evening and taken 50 pounds of cocaine, 155 pounds of marijuana, 20 pounds of methamphetamine, 5 pounds of ecstasy, 10 fully automatic assault weapons, and the lowly .45 caliber revolver.

Tomorrow, I will use it to kill the traitor, he thought. The ricin would take a couple days to kill its victim. Roland was glad that it was a rare event and would make headlines and television news. He would get to watch in joy seeing his handy work. But, the gun, the gun was more personal. Roland shook with excitement thinking about how the traitor would beg for his miserable life.

He would go to the rally tomorrow. Following the traitor when he left the rally, Roland would hold him up at gun point near the turncoat's car, force him to drive them to a secluded place out of town, and shoot him dead. The body would then simply "disappear" due to one of Roland's connections in the underworld. Roland smiled at the miniature movie of the event playing out in his head.

There were a couple of assumptions that made Roland's plan flawed. First, the traitor didn't own a car and rode to the rally with his gay friend, Dan. Second, the traitor did not plan to go to the rally on its last day. The hetero ally who loved equality had other stuff to do that day. Little did Roland know.

...

I got out of my urine-soaked clothes and headed to work. With flexible hours, I had set myself for a short shift today. In four hours, I would head to my doctor's appointment. After the doctor, I was officially on vacation.

I hadn't taken vacation in over two years. That's not to say I didn't use my vacation time. Last year, my vacation time was used to help tend to my ailing mother. She would die two days after I returned to work that year. So it goes. The year before I had planned a trip to France, but my sister's son was quite ill. My sister was a single mother and had a dead end job. Many people had such jobs in these economic times. She was underpaid and overworked and had little vacation time to spare. I took my vacation to cover watching over the young one. Unlike my mother, my niece didn't die. She recovered a day before I left

Chicago to head back to Boston. This year was my turn. I was going to enjoy my vacation for once.

My plan was to use the first three or four days to unpack and adjust to my new condo. Finishing that, I would rent a car and drive across the country to see not only its lovely sights but to meet up with long lost friends and relatives. After reaching the terminus of my drive, I would fly back from Los Angeles to Boston. I had a little over two weeks, and I was going to enjoy it.

My work badge was on the table. I would have had to come home to get it even if I hadn't pissed myself. Grabbing it, I left and headed to work.

•••

Although most of Roland's worth was invested in companies that he himself did not run, Roland did direct the dealings of one company. It was a small conglomerate of dairy farms that he had bought below market value. They had needed an investor, and, at the time, he had needed a hobby. Its revenue streams were modest. The company was called Queen of the Prairies Dairy Delights of Manchester. For marketing, they used only the first half of the lengthy company name. One of their posters looked like this:

QUEEN OF THE PRAIRIES

Roland sat at his desk and viewed his assets on his computers screen. The total worth still exceeded a number with nine zeros, but he was beginning to feel a little nervous as it had decreased steadily over the last quarter. He was about to call his financial service advisor to talk to him about how he could shift his assets to get a better return. The phone rang. Few people had the number to his mancave, so he picked up.

"Hey, Travis, it's Shane," the adolescent voice expressed with jolly.

"Kid, you have the wrong number," Roland said.

"Com'n, Travis, I know it's you," the young male said teasingly.

"No, kid, I'm not *fucking* Travis."

"I know you aren't, Jennifer is!," the snarky kid retorted and hung up. Wrong number.

Roland was mad at how the kid had talked to him, but he had to laugh at the kid's quick wit. Setting the phone down, Roland briefly reflected on his youth and his two parents who had died in an accident on their way to get him at baseball practice.

The phone rang again.

"I'm not Travis, you little punk," Roland answered.

Confused, Willard Jones, said, "Uh, I'm trying to reach Mr. Roland."

"Sorry, Willard," Roland responded.
Willard was his right hand man when it came to the Queen of the Prairies enterprise. He informed Roland that due to some decrease in production caused by a fire at one of the larger dairy farms of the conglomerate, they were going to need some reinvestment by Roland. The farm had tried to boost production by storing more fertilizer than was allowed by regulation. The fertilizer would help the grass and clover grow even faster than normal. Fertilizer had high levels of ammonium nitrate and was combustible. At the farm, an incompetent worker had decided to have a smoke break near the fertilizer. The worker, 38 cows, and the building were no more. So it goes.

...

"By the way, you have to cover," my coworker said to me as I passed her on my way to my office.

"Really?" I replied.

"Braydon, Theresa, and Maria are all at appointments, Becca took her maternity leave early, Kyle is in the hospital, and Regina is out sick," she informed me.

I would have to cover the Spanish calls during my shift. It was one of the many classes I had taken in college on my way to *not* earning a degree.

"Is Kyle okay?" I asked.

"Trying to better his career, he went quail hunting with Kaney, yesterday." Kaney was the VP of the company.

"Kaney accidentally shot him in the face, but don't worry all signs say that Kyle will be good as new in about five days," my coworker reported.

"That's good to know," I responded.

I headed to my office and set the phone to take both English and Spanish speaking clients. My Spanish was rusty, but, as the train tracks of my life would have it, I was the best Spanish speaker in the office for the day.

The phone rang.

"Hello, Imagination Financial Services, how can I help you, today?" I answered with a smile. Unlike many businesses, Imagination did not use an acronym for its name. They were probably worried that customers would see too much risk in investing if the place was called IFS.

I helped the customer with their issue and turned my computer on. The phone rang again.

"Hello, Imagination Financial Services, how can I help you, today?" I answered with a smile.

"It's me," the voice responded with a giggle.

I sat up straight in my chair.

"Blossom, how are you?"

"I'm good, just thought I'd squeeze in a call today." I had given her my business card with my work number and cell number on it. I didn't have a home number set up yet in my condo, and I wasn't sure if I was going to pay for a phone when my cell would do just fine.

Since I was only unpacking for the next three days or so, I decided to ask if she could see me in the coming days.

"Sorry," she said sadly, "my parents are coming by to get me. We're heading to Maine because my aunt is not well."

"Sorry to hear that," I said, "I hope she gets better."

"Let's hope," she replied. After talking more, we realized that our paths would not cross until I arrived back in Boston from my vacation. We stopped trying to plan the future and simply enjoyed a conversation.

My supervisor came in my office.

"We are backlogged with Spanish speakers, you need to be more efficient with your calls," he commanded. With over 34 million Spanish speakers in the United States and our company actively marketing to them, it was obvious that I was going to have a busy last day before my vacation.

Blossom overheard him. "I'll let you go," she said, "but see you when you get back."

...

Roland now had to call his financial broker, Braydon Winfield, for two reasons. First, he wanted to reorganize his portfolio to be more aggressive in generating revenue. Second, Roland needed to transfer some funds to the account used by the Queen of the Prairies, Inc. He hoped it would not take long because he had an appointment with a shady individual soon.

He dialed Braydon's direct line and was transferred to an automated system. Roland didn't call Braydon often. Being a billionaire, he had Braydon's cell number to call. But, Roland forgot that fact and listened to the automated system.

"Press 1 for English, Pulse dos para español," the robot voice commanded.

Roland intended to press one, but, not realizing it, had selected two.

He was on hold listening to salsa music. Fucking spicks, he thought, I can't even call and talk about my money without having to hear their music. Luckily, I don't have to listen to their gibberish.

...

As soon as I set the phone down from Blossom's call, it rang.

"Hola, ¿cómo puedo ayudarlo a usted, hoy?" I said with a smile.

"Do you know how to speak American or English, you..." the voice faded. He was going to call the speaker a "spick," but he always composed himself and hid his true beliefs as to not gain unwanted media attention. Billionaires had a public image to maintain.

"Sorry," I said, "I'm taking calls for English and Spanish, today."

"How can I help you, sir?" I added.

"I'm trying to get ahold of Braydon Winfield," the voice replied. That voice was queerly familiar, but I couldn't place it.

"He's out at an appointment right now, can I help you?" I asked.

"Nah, I only deal with him, can you leave him a message?" the voice responded.

"Sure"

"Tell him, Kevin Dewayne Roland called and get back to me asap"

"I will," I promised.

···

As Roland hung up the phone, he had the strange feeling he knew that voice. He racked his brain trying to recall who it was. The memory of the previous day's interaction with the traitor didn't come. Yet.

···

I finished my bilingual, cover shift having only made a few minor errors with my Spanish. Locating my supervisor, I told him I was leaving and my vacation was beginning. He was often absent-minded, and I didn't want him calling tomorrow when I didn't show. I wanted to sleep in. It had been a long day, and it was not over yet. The doctor appointment was still waiting for me.

My doctor's office was across town, so I went to the closest bus stop and waited. I sat down and tried to relax.

A thought bubble burst in my mind. I shook in pain. The older lady next to me on the bus bench thought I was having a seizure. Instead of trying to help she scooted down the bench to create distance. She didn't want to catch what I had.

I didn't even know what I had. Maybe, it was contagious, but I had not seen another person who I interacted with come down with the symptoms. I

144

doubted it was contagious. The bubble pierced my brain. It felt like someone had put a knitting needle in a fire, taken it out glowing hot, and shoved it through my ear into my brain. I sobbed slightly and tried to compose myself as I shook.

Taking the notepad out and one of the four pens I made sure to keep with me now, I started to write. The words came easy:

Merriam Beauveax was a middle-aged, French immigrant who had readied herself for the project's arrival by dressing as if to go to a nightclub.

I wrote only two handwritten pages and the feeling passed. Though I hated the pain, a piece of me was hoping the event would transpire when I was at the doctor's so they could see it occur.

The bus stopped and opened its doors. The little, old lady, who was so afraid of whatever the hell I had, rushed like an Olympic sprinter to get on the bus before me. At the rate she moved, she would have likely won a bronze at the 1972 Olympics. If she had, her reward would have looked like this:

It was amazing how fast people could move when they were afraid.

I got on the bus and made sure to sit next to the little, old lady. She cowered to get closer to the window.

...

The waiting room of the doctor's office had a number of magazines. The magazines were there to help to pass the time for people who were waiting. No one was reading any of them. The other patients were on their phones playing games or texting. I picked up a magazine. The magazine focused on psychology, culture, and speculation. I skimmed its table of contents and found that Klondyke Bass had written an article. Bass was known for his science fiction writing. I had read a few of his books including *Gorge and Go Green*. This article was outside his normal genre.

In the article entitled *A Broken Man*, Bass speculated on the recent activity and statements of a Senator named Aiken Todd. The article postulated that Todd's actions were in line with people who suffer from PTSD or Post-Traumatic Stress Disorder. Since the Senator had never served in combat, Bass claimed that the PTSD was linked to some other new event in the man's life. Noting research on the behavioral shift in women who have been victims of rape, Bass argued that the Senator was likely a survivor of rape. Either he was raped at a young age and the memories had come to surface, Bass asserted, or he was a victim quite recently.

I was quite a fan of Bass's science fiction but didn't enjoy the article. It was not a genre Bass should be writing in. I couldn't buy his arguments and doubted that Todd was a victim of rape. Little did I know.

The nurse called my name, and I headed back to meet with the doctor.

...

Roland left his home as Mr. Clay Johnson, another costume within Roland's vast repertoire. He had one goal left to complete his day's events. Roland had poisoned one of his targets and had taken care of his financial matters. Now, it was time to focus on the plan for killing the other target, the traitor.

Roland met with an individual named Casey Jones. Jones lived in the ghetto of Ilium, and Roland always felt uncomfortable surrounded by so diverse of a population. Roland knocked on Jones' door. A tall well-built and heavily tattooed male came to the door.

He opened the door. "Come on in, Clay," he said.

"I don't have a lot of time," Roland replied.

"Okay, I have what you want, but you sure you don't need anything else," Jones asked. Jones was anxious to do more business with Clay Johnson because he paid well beyond the market value for items.

"Not that I can think of, but I'll contact you again if something comes up," Roland responded.

Jones led Clay to a back room and pulled out a case. In the case was a .45 caliber revolver of the same model as the one possessed by Roland, six special rounds, and a silencer.

Roland interrupted Jones who had started to talk, "I don't need the gun or bullets, I just wanted the silencer."

"Since you're such a good customer," Jones replied, "I was throwing in the gun, bullets, and case."

Jones went on, "The bullets are special and can be hard to find. They're armor piercing."

"Okay," Clay proclaimed, "I'll take all of it but the pistol. I don't want it."

Roland left the house with the case with the silencer and armor piercing bullets and headed home. Tomorrow, the traitor will die, and I will enjoy watching him take his last breath, Roland thought as he drove away.

...

Dr. Sandra Foote came into the examination room. She asked me how I was and called me by my first name.

"Overall, good," I answered, "but I'm having some strange issue."

I explained to her the pain and shaking, the sweating and nausea, the burning up while being electrocuted sensation. After explaining all the symptoms, I told Dr. Foote that I had found temporary relief by writing or typing the thoughts in my head.

She began examining me. Checking my reflexes, she said, "did it affect your breathing?"

"No, not that I'm aware."

"How about your eye sight?"

"No, not that I know"

She looked into my eyes and ears with her otoscope.

"Did they feel like hallucinations?"

"No, just pain, just god awful pain. I didn't 'see' anything. I didn't even know what I was thinking until I got to a piece of paper or computer to write it."

I told Dr. Foote that the pain and drive was so great that I had pissed myself earlier. Given a choice between going to the bathroom and getting out the words, I had chosen the words. It was only the second time I got embarrassed to tell her about my medical situation. A couple years ago, I told her I thought I had an STD. STD stood for sexually transmitted disease. Medicine loved acronyms. Turned out, I only had a serious, urinary tract infection.

Dr. Foote finished her thorough examination.

"So?" I asked, "what is it?"

"Whatever is happening to you is not physical. Or, at least, it isn't anything that I have ever heard of or seen."

I trusted her. It must not be physical then because Dr. Foote was one of the top medical doctors in the area and had practiced medicine for more than 20 years.

"So?" I asked again.

"I think it may be psychological," she said tenderly being careful not to appear judgmental.

"You mean I'm *crazy*," I said raising my voice slightly.

She explained that there were a number of neurotic and psychotic conditions that people dealt with that didn't mean they were "crazy." Depression and anxiety were common conditions that had psychological roots and did not mean the person was "crazy."

Dr. Foote gave me the contact information of a psychologist that she recommended. She informed me that, given my upcoming vacation, she would call now and get an appointment for me. Dr. Foote took out her cell and dialed her friend. In a matter of minutes, I had an appointment for tomorrow.

As I left her office, Dr. Foote turned to me smiling and said, "The next time I see you, I will be able to say, 'you were sick, but now you're well, and there's work to do."

ELEVEN

Vonnegut walked into the lab and stumbled. He didn't fall to the floor, but something was affecting his equilibrium.

"You okay?" a technician asked sincerely.

"I'll be fine," Vonnegut replied, "I just need to get this book done."

"Your writing a book?" the technician inquired.

"It's already written in my mind," Vonnegut asserted. "Just hook me to that machine," he added pointing to the TT machine.

The technician and two assistants did just that. After the halo was in place, they turned on the TT machine. It rattled and hummed. Vonnegut began thinking:

Roland hobbled through the crowd, but he saw no sign of the traitor or the dark-skinned man that was next to the traitor yesterday.

By the time the machine turned off, Vonnegut had completed his final novel.

...

Joe Lazzaro, who had said, "PU, you stink," to Vonnegut in the van that had brought them to the TT facility, was babbling. The guard in Lazzaro's wing of the TT facility walked down to listen the commotion. He leaned close to the door to listen in.

"Bike ramps are cool, but bags on your head are not"

"Green Eggs and Ham stole my thoughts," said the voice in the room.

"Leonard Hayes won't miss the watch I stole, but this facility sure is lonely," Lazzaro claimed.

"My tree house is better than your secret government facility," it went on.

The guard thought that he was misunderstanding the words. He stuck his finger in his ears to see if he could clean out any wax that may be corrupting his comprehension of the sounds. Listening again, he was sure it was not his ears.

"Mom, can I have a...two men came to the door to get me"

"I promise I won't pee the bed again; I hate the pot roast here, should have gotten the hamburger."

The guard was sure he was no mistaken in what he had heard. He left to report the crazy mumblings to his superior. And so on.

...

Lazzaro's door opened and three guards stood at its edge. They were unsure if he would be violent, so they decided to not risk it and bring more people than was needed. The guards were there to escort him to the infirmary and have him examined.

Lazzaro smiled.

"Give me the popsicle, I was in Vietnam, this cot is too hard," he said to the guards. All of Lazzaro's other statements, while odd, were not lies. This one was the exception. Lazzaro had never been in Vietnam. He was three years old at the peak of the conflict, but it was a lie he told to women when he tried to pick them up at a bar. Some knew enough history that it didn't work, but others blindly listened to his false heroics. Like you, I hate being lied to.

...

Any of the historically-challenged women who came home with Lazzaro for the night would find a bomb with the words "Ashes in a Moment" written on it. He would tell him that he had found it while on patrol in Vietnam and had brought it back after the war. It looked like this:

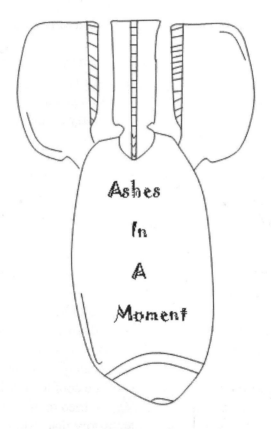

But, the fact was he bought it at an Army surplus store. Like you, I hate being lied to.

...

But to continue:

The senior guard asked Lazzaro to come with them. Lazzaro did. There was no conflict. Lazzaro was just glad to be getting out of his room.

The doctors at the infirmary ran a number of tests on Lazzaro. At first, they thought that it was a psychological issue. After reading the test results of his brain scan, they realized that he had a unique stroke. The TT machine had fused synaptic junctions in his brain in such a way as to have him blend memories and words of his distant past with experience in the present.

Having seen a number of physical abnormalities in the participants, the doctors reported Lazzaro's issue to Dr. Heath. It was the 432nd different issue they had found in the research participants. The TT machine caused adverse affects to each participant. It seems you cannot steal a person's thoughts without it impacting them in some way.

...

The TT technicians removed the halo from Vonnegut's head. He was done.

Vonnegut heard a mumbling and turned his head to the right to try to locate it.

"You can get out of the chair now," the technician repeated.

Vonnegut couldn't hear out of his right ear. At least not well, that is.

"Thanks," he said as he stood up. His first step from the chair sent him crashing to the floor. Two technicians rushed to help him up.

"Are you okay?" the one on the left asked. Vonnegut rubbed his ears before shaking his head no. His right ear felt heavy as if he was being weighed down by something. He needed to find a mirror to get perspective. Vonnegut felt like he was tilting his head to the right side no matter how he moved his neck to adjust. His left ear burned and hummed.

"Something's wrong with my ears," he told them.

"Let's get him to the infirmary," the lead technician stated.

...

Vonnegut had to focus immensely to walk normally. He followed a guard to the infirmary.

Walking into the infirmary, he passed a young man sitting on an examination table.

"Mom, can you cut the peanut butter and jelly sandwich in half, so I can ride in that 2007 Voyager," the man told Vonnegut. It was Joe Lazzaro. Vonnegut wondered what was wrong with the man.

The doctors ran all the tests that they had previously ran on Lazzaro and a few others. Vonnegut was a celebrity, and they needed to know if the TT machine had done something to him. In fact, the machine had stimulated his body in such a way as to cause him to thicken the fluid in his ear. That fluid was not only more viscous than it should be but would also continue to thicken over the coming days. Vonnegut had a unique disorder that was most closely related to Meniere Disease. It would affect his balance. If one lost their ability to balance at an inappropriate time like near a road with heavy traffic or at the top of a staircase, it could be deadly. Before telling Vonnegut their diagnosis, they made sure to report to Heath.

"Under no circumstances are you to tell him," Heath demanded. The lead doctor left Heath's office and began thinking of what to tell Vonnegut.

...

The lead doctor returned to Vonnegut's examination table.

"Mr. Vonnegut," the doctor started, "it appears that your blood sugar is low and you are tired from a long day." It was a lie. Like you, I hate being lied to.

The doctor went on, "These factors can cause people to feel light-headed and, even, affect their balance. As it did in your case."

"But my ears," Vonnegut began but was interrupted by the doctor.

"We will drain your ear wax, now, because the low blood sugar may have increased its production, and we will send a large meal to your room that I suggest you eat."

The doctors did as they had said and drained Vonnegut's ear wax. Even though it was not the central issue, Vonnegut noticed a slight difference, but that change would only buy him time. The adverse affects Vonnegut suffered to get his last novel written would likely be the cause of his demise. So it, kinda sorta, goes.

TWELVE

Roland woke up late. His expensive alarm clock had malfunctioned. He was an hour behind the schedule he had set for the day and irritated that he would start the day on the wrong foot. Roland got out of bed and rushed to the bathroom to clean up. His compulsion to hurry was driven as much by his waking late as his excitement in knowing that he would hunt down the traitor today. Originally, he had planned to be at the rally early because he expected that the traitor would spend the entire day there. That bastard. The traitor would force Roland to stand in that retched pile of useless faggots. He shuttered at the thought of being surrounded by men who might undress him with their eyes. As he showered, Roland decided to change which character he was going to play. Instead of Luke Taylor, he would be Jenna Thompson. Roland thought he could handle the lesbians in the group hitting on him, but what Roland didn't account for were the gay men who had heightened their awareness of what men dressed as women looked like.

...

I woke late. Having no work or significant time obligations outside of my late afternoon appointment with a psychologist, I hadn't even set my poorly manufactured alarm clock. I felt refreshed. The remote for my television was on the nightstand near my bed. I turned on the TV.

The last time I was watching this TV in my condo I had been watching a 24-hour news network, so the news came on as the TV lit up.

"Yes, he is a public defender," one the commentators of the 'expert' panel was saying to the reporter. The image on the screen was a picture of JJ. I sat up straight in the bed.

"A pretty good one from his record," another commentator added. In this 24-hour news cycle, it was getting harder and harder to tell the difference between commentators, reporters, experts, journalists, and hobos with an opinion. In fact, calling some of the individuals who came to such shows "hobos with an opinion" was generous. Hobos had a code of ethics.

I was shaken as I discovered from the newscast that JJ had been poisoned and was in critical condition. Many of his organs were failing, and doctors had no cure.

The news segment concluded by informing the audience that if they had seen Juan Jackson in the last 24 hours to notify police as they may be a key witness to crime. Until that moment in the newscast, I was unaware that he had been *deliberately* poisoned.

I jumped out of bed and ran over to my cellphone on the charger. Who knows, maybe I could help the police. I called them.

...

Roland took the voice modulator out of the dog tags it was in and placed it into a locket. He had learned from his previous error. Adjusting the settings, he practiced talking and listening to the quality of the vocals as they shifted to more and more feminine in nature. He had never dressed as Jenna before and was looking for the voice that would match the costume.

He finished the adjustment and his look. Grabbing the purse that had the loaded .45 in it, he headed to the garage. Switching the plates of the F150 from Texas back to Tennessee, he headed out.

The sky was grey and a steady rain hit the windshield. Roland hoped that it would not dissuade the traitor from making it to the rally.

...

The police informed me that they were aware that I had been with JJ yesterday. They had been analyzing all available video surveillance in the area as well as talking to other witnesses at the rally. In fact, the officer on the phone informed me that a detective was in route and should have already arrived.

"If your calling from your residence at 116 Heritage Park, stay there, he will be there any minute," the officer on the phone told me.

"Sir, that's the wrong address, I recently moved," I replied. After telling him my new address, he told me to wait there and someone would come to see me.

"We have *a lot* of questions for you," he said in a tone that felt accusatory.

"I will, sir, I will."

...

As Jenna Thompson, Roland entered the crowd at the rally holding a pink umbrella over his head to keep the rain from getting him wet. The rain was not heavy but steady. It had affected the turnout. Less people were on both sides of the street.

Roland scanned the crowd looking for the despicable traitor.

Roland believed he had seen everyone in the crowd. Had he missed him? Had the coward shied away from the rally because of the rain? Roland didn't know, but he was going to wait to see if that monster showed his face. As time passed, Roland grew more disheartened that the traitor would not show his face. Roland's mood matched the hue of the overcast day.

A police officer was coming Roland's way. Act natural, stay calm, he told himself. The officer stopped at the person next him. Roland could overhear the conversation. They were interviewing people to see if they had been there yesterday when Juan Jackson was poisoned. The officer finished his conversation with the woman to Roland's left.

"Excuse me," he said to Roland, "were you hear yesterday?"

"Oh, no," said Roland, in a feminine voice thanks to the modulator, "I just got into town."

"Did you come for the rally?"

"No, I have relatives here that I'm visiting." It was a lie. Like you, I hate to be lied to.

"So, you thought while you were visiting you would come down here and support this cause."

"Oh my, no," Roland protested, "I don't take sides. I just wanted to see what all the fuss was about."

Happy with the answers, the officer moved on to question others. Roland desperately scanned the crowd again. Where the hell was the son of a bitch? He thought.

Someone bumped him, and Roland stumbled to find his balance in his high heels.

"Sorry miss....ter?" the guy said, "I didn't see you."

"It's okay," Roland said.

That was now the third time that someone had either bumped into him or excused themselves as they passed in front of him. In each case, they had all called Roland "miss...ter." Roland wondered who this Ms. Ter was. Did his Jenna custom happen to look like some famous lesbian? He thought. In fact, some gay men had become accustomed to distinguishing a woman from a man in drag and knew that Roland was a man playing a woman.

...

In actuality, most members, in the gay community, would not even use the Miss and Mister labels with a stranger. Most would have simply have said sorry. Binary categories were counter to the range of subject positions people in the community held.

...

But to continue:

The last rally member to bump Roland and say "sorry miss...ter" did more than have him think of some fictitious character named Ms. Ter. It also triggered a memory. The memory was of the traitor bumping into him yesterday at the rally. That, that was the voice on the telephone that he couldn't place before. The traitor worked for Imagination Financial Services. Could it be? Could such an act be mere coincidence? It was a sign from the Creator of the Universe that Roland needed to find that traitor and make him pay for his sins.

Now, Roland didn't have to hunt him down in this pack of rainbow-wearing weirdos. He could hunt the traitor by following him after work. Roland didn't remember the traitor's name, but he knew he could get that from his financial advisor, Braydon.

The rain had nearly passed. He closed the umbrella as he left the rally. Roland smiled as he climbed into the F150. Things were looking up.

...

I hung up the phone. The police would be here soon. Did I have time to take a quick shower? I thought. I wanted to be presentable when they arrived. Rushing into the bathroom, I turned the shower on. I left the bathroom door open, so I could hear a knock if it came. It didn't take me long to clean up, I should be okay, I thought.

I rubbed the shampoo into my scalp. Dandruff had become an issue for me lately, and the special shampoo was supposed to help. It burned. I heard something. I paused. They were knocking on my door. Geez, what an inopportune time, I thought. I rushed to rinse the shampoo and jumped out of the shower. Drying off, I wrapped a white towel around my waist and hurried to the door.

...

Chris and Lidia Heyward needed some more cash. Their child was sick, and the hospital bills were killing them. The only person they knew with disposable income lived in a condo on the other side of town. This would not be their first trip to see him. They had "borrowed" almost $10,000 from him in the last few months. He was financially comfortable, and they knew he didn't really expect it back. They needed more. Gathering their sick daughter and their other four kids, they hopped a bus to go give the philanthropist a surprise visit. If they called, he might avoid them. That had happened once before.

...

The knocking appeared urgent. It came again, fast and hard. I rushed to my door in my towel. After answering, I thought, I would just excuse myself and let the officer in.

I opened the door, and my towel fell to the floor. In my rush, I had not tucked it in tight enough, and the quick motions to the door had worked it free. Naked, I stood before a man, woman, and five kids.

Two police officers, a male and a female, came to my door as I reached down to get the towel quickly.

The male officer said, "For god's sake, cover yourself, man." He was stating the obvious. I had already grabbed the towel and was wrapping it around me again.

Turning to the Heywards, the female officer asked, "Do you know this man?"

"No, but," Lidia Heyward had put two and two together, having seen all my boxes in the background, "our friend used to live here and must have moved."

The Heywards left, and the two officers came inside. I asked the officers to have a seat and give me a second to get dressed. I hurried to my bedroom and got some clothes on.

...

Roland got to his home and was sitting on his couch. He had opened a bottle of 1996 Chteau Lafite. Roland didn't usually drink during the day, but he felt that he should open one of the bottles and enjoy the news coverage of his act.

"The medical team is considering all available options, but the outlook is grim for Mr. Jackson" the anchor announced.

Roland could only smile as he drank his glass of wine.

...

No need for socks or shoes, I thought, and threw on a pair of jeans and a t-shirt. I walked into the living room and sat in the chair facing the two officers on the couch.

"So," the female officer started, "yesterday you went to the rally with Juan Jackson?"

"No," I answered, "I went with my friend Dan to the rally."

"But you met up with Mr. Jackson at the rally?" the male questioned.

"I didn't plan to," I responded, "but I was glad to see him again." I was sweating. Even though I had done nothing wrong, I was nervous.

"How did you know Mr. Jackson exactly," the female officer chimed in, again.

"Well, I just met him the day before yesterday, on the first day of the rally."

"And.." she drew out, encouraging me to continue.

"He was friendly and wanted some coffee, so we had some coffee, and he told me a little about his past."

"Did anyone harass him while you were together?" the male, now, asked.

I paused trying to reflect on the last two days. The male officer took my lengthy pause with suspicion. His last three wives had cheated on him. He was suspicious of anyone who violated his expectations. He decided to press me.

"You know, we've seen video surveillance from the coffee shop," he stated bluntly.

"Yeah," I replied questioningly.

"A tall, White gentleman in a beanie stopped at your table and talked to you two for a minute. What did he say?"

"Oh, that guy, that guy only asked JJ where he had bought his shirt, said he liked it and wanted one," I recalled.

"And the incident the next day?" the officer asked, holding back a smile.

"I, um, I," I stuttered, "I pissed myself."

"We saw that on the tape," the female officer asserted, "why?"

"It's an issue I am trying to understand. I went to the doctor yesterday, and have an appointment with a psychologist later today." I regretted saying psychologist and should have just said specialist.

"So, you have a mental illness," the female said tenderly.

"I don't know. I just don't know."

The officers continued to question me for another half an hour and, then, left. They had already placed me high on the suspect list. With the added information about my mental state and psychologist appointment, they would place me on the top of that list.

...

After the police left, I got some food and began unpacking boxes. I had to get some of this done before my trip. There were a few items in this clutter that I planned to take with me. I turned on the TV to see if there were any updates on JJ's condition. The reporter, in a morose tone, stated, "The medical team is considering all available options, but the outlook is grim for Mr. Jackson."

I felt like the view out my window, grey and glum. The rain had stopped earlier, but the overcast was depressing. The scene from my condo was like a gothic painting on valium.

As I continued to work on my packages, I found most of the items I needed to take on my trip. An old book of poems written by my mother was there. I needed to hand-deliver it to my sister in Chicago. It was the only remaining copy that we knew of. I placed the book on the couch. Next, I located the Beatles' Sgt. Pepper album, which I had bought as a gift for my buddy in Kansas City. He collected vinyl albums and had been searching for this one for some time. Luckily, I found it at a garage sale six months ago. I put the album on the couch next to the book. Last, I found my gun case. I unzipped it. There was my grandfather's double-barreled, 12 gauge shotgun. My Kansas City buddy wanted to go hunting when I stopped in next. He liked to hunt anything, and my 12 gauge was pretty versatile. I only needed to get the right ammunition. Zipping the gun case up, I set it next to the couch.

As I opened the last box that I planned to unpack before heading to my doctor's appointment, I heard the TV anchor.

"Mr. Juan Jackson is now in a coma," the reporter noted, "he is not expected to recover. Our thoughts are with his family."

I cried. Though I had not known him long, I felt a connection to him. His spirit had made me feel at home in a crowd that was quite different from me. His stories had showed me that one should persevere. I called out to the Creator of the Universe, "Please don't let him die." It was in vain.

"This just in, Mr. Jackson, has succumb to his condition," the TV announced. So it goes.

...

With JJ heavy on my mind, I headed to my appointment with Dr. Ryan Brane. My brain shifted focus from the depression and emotion that I was feeling from JJ's death to a cold, analytical mindset. I let my mind replay all the events of the rally, and I dissected them bit by bit. The man with the Winchester cap, the coffee shop, the barista, the guy asking JJ about his shirt, Dan, the reporter named Che, the guy whose laptop I rented, Blossom, the other barista, the guy with the crutches, the intern who forgot the camera, all ran threw my mind.

"You getting in," a voice called.

I was standing at the bus stop to go to the Brane appointment. Unable to grasp where I was briefly, I responded, "Huh?"

"Are you getting in?" the bus driver's voice boomed.

"Yeah, sorry," I said as I boarded.

...

I got to my appointment with Dr. Brane right on time. He took me into his office.

"Have a seat anywhere you like" he stated.

There were four chairs and two couches in the room. I wondered if where I sat had meaning to the psychologist. If I sat in the far chair, I may be sending a message that I was distant and didn't trust him already. I decided to sit on the end of the couch closest to the chair near the desk that I assumed he would sit in. He sat down in it.

"So, my colleague told me that I needed to see you. Do you want to tell me the issue?"

This was not an issue about trust and sharing secrets. It was about finding answers. I explained all the events that were happening to me.

"You felt so compelled to write that you urinated on yourself," Dr. Brane stated, looking for me to confirm.

"Yeah, I don't know what has gotten into me."

Dr. Brane turned to his desk, looked through his business card holder, selected a card, and turned back to face me.

"I have good news and bad," he said softly.

"Okay?" I mumbled.

"I'm not sure I can help you, but I would try if you wanted me to. However," he took a deep breath, "I'm pretty sure this guy can help you."

He handed me the business card.

Brane went on, "I listened to a lecture he gave once that suggests that he may have worked with individuals with your unique problem. I'm not positive he can help, but he is a renown neuropsychologist who is about to retire. You should make an appointment with him soon."

Our session concluded. As I left the office, I looked at the card:

DR. DARNELL DURLING HEATH, Neuropsychologist & Neurophysicist

...

The thing is:

Examining my writing and seeing the names Vonnegut, Merriam Beauveax, and Voyager, Heath would have been able to piece together my strange issue. He would connect them all to the TT project he had directed years ago. Heath was the only living person who could understand and, potentially, fix my problem. However, that would never occur. My HMO did not authorize me to see such a specialist. My health insurance company cared more about their bottom dollar than my well-being. They would not spend the additional money on me, so I never met Heath. I dealt with the issue alone.

THIRTEEN

Listen:

Roland was dead set on killing the traitor on the day following the death of Juan Jackson. The traitor would not die that day. Roland had pressing issues he had to take care of. A company called Nabe Capital was attempting a hostile takeover of the Queen of the Prairies. Nabe didn't make anything. They just bought weakened businesses and restructured them. Sometimes, the restructured company was stronger. Other times, they failed and everyone connected to the company were left unemployed. Roland didn't especially care for his company, but he was adamant that if it failed it would be at his hands rather than theirs. The attempted takeover was more theatrical. There was no bane for the Queen. After a day of intense, legal maneuvering, the Queen of the Prairies was safe.

...

I woke the day after JJ had died. Doing some research, I found which foundation JJ had listed in his will for sending donations in his name. I filled out a check and sent it. His lose was still heavy on me. I desperately hoped the police would locate the party responsible and shot him on the spot. They wouldn't, of course. Criminals had the right to a fair and speedy trial. Well, unless they were a cop killer, then they merely found their end in a blaze of glory with other cops.

As I unpacked more boxes in a feeble attempt to complete the task before my vacation the following day, I felt it. I was getting accustomed to the sensation. The event was building in my body. There was no pain or shaking yet. I rushed to my desk and readied to type. Bam! An explosion of thought burst in my mind, and I starting typing. The first line said:

"Greene, Tyler Greene," Roland said in huff."

The thought bubble passed.

What the hell? I thought.

All the previous typing I had done related to frat boys, a French woman, Vonnegut, and Voyager minivans. This, this was different. It was more like a memory. In fact, it was a memory. My recollection of the day of JJ's death came back to me more vivid than when I had discussed it with the police. Tyler Greene was the man with the crutch who kept crowding us. I remembered an eerie sensation I had when I saw him. Getting up from the desk, I walked across the room, got the phone, and called the police.

As I waited on hold to speak with a detective working the case, my mind raced. Did I know Tyler Greene? Why did the sentence have the name Roland in it? Was Roland a typo? I was pretty sure I didn't know anyone named Roland. Unfortunately, I was thinking of Roland as a first name. I had certainly heard of Kevin Dwayne Roland. Everyone had. He was not only a well-known and respected billionaire but a client of Imagination Financial Services where I worked. If only my mind would have contemplated the word "Roland" as a last name, I may have made the connection. My mind lingered on the precipice of knowing, but the thought died. So it goes.

...

By the time Roland finished defending his company from a hostile takeover, it was late in the day. He called his financial broker, Braydon, anyway. Roland left a detailed message asking about the individual who spoke with him on the phone the other day. He instructed Braydon to contact him as soon as possible because he had enjoyed the service and wanted to send the guy a "thank you" gift.

...

But to continue:

The detective thanked me for my insight. She told me that the guy with the crutch was a prime suspect. The police department's face recognition software could not determine who he was due to the angle of the surveillance images and his sunglasses. With the name "Tyler Greene," they would make headway in the case, she assured me.

I hung up the phone feeling good that I had potentially led the police to JJ's killer. Since I was leaving on vacation the next day, I decided that unpacking my many boxes would have to wait. I needed to actually pack my bags for my trip.

Going into my bedroom, I went into my walk in closet and got my luggage. One was larger. I used it the last two years on my trips to see my mom and, then, my sister. The other was smaller. The last time I needed it was when my entire family met for the holidays.

I opened the smaller one. It was not empty. Two cards were there. The first looked like this:

Before opening and reading it, I knew it was from my dad. He was quite religious. Noel means birthday. The card was a birthday card because the holiday was to celebrate the birth of Jesus Christ. It was not my birthday. Mine was in April. But, I got the birthday card anyways.

My dad would talk about Jesus being the sacrificial lamb. A lamb looked like this:

For the longest time, I thought the sacrificial element was the stealing of the sheep's wool. The sheep would sacrifice its coat so we could have sweaters, mittens, hats, and such. Not long ago, I was told it was used in ancient times as a blood sacrifice. It seems you had to slaughter something to show just how much you cared. The other card looked like this:

SEASON'S GREETINGS

I already knew it was from my brother. He was an atheist. No card from him would be a Jesus' birthday card. No Noel, No Merry Christmas, just kind words near the Winter solstice. No lambs had to die for him. He was a vegan.

...

The next day, early in the morning, Roland got his awaited call from Braydon. The financial advisor told Roland all he knew about the traitor including his name, his address at his new condo, and his hobbies. Braydon thought he was doing his peer a service. He thought the billionaire would reward his peer with a generous gift. The only thing on Roland's mind was killing that vile individual.

Roland made up his mind to dress as Luke Taylor and shoot the traitor in his own home. The gun was nearly untraceable. With the silencer, it would make little noise to alert neighbors of the incident.

Luke was a character that Roland had been anticipating playing. He had tattoo sleeves, an earring, deep brown eyes, and a menacing body. Of course,

Roland didn't have the muscles that the body suit depicted, but he knew that the sight of Luke was intimidating to many people. Roland hoped the traitor would shake with fear at the sight of the muscle-bound character.

Roland loaded the .45 with the armor piercing rounds. Might as well get my money's worth, he thought, as he slid the sixth and final cartridge into the cylinder. He screwed the silencer onto the barrel and set the weapon down. Because of their design, most revolvers didn't really become silent with a silencer. The revolver Roland owned was a rare exception. Roland headed to the costume section of his mancave to get ready. He couldn't wait.

...

The day of the start of my vacation came. I woke happy that I would get a much needed break. After showering, I got dressed. All my gear lay on the couch. The large suitcase, small suitcase, gym bag, and shotgun case sat patiently waiting for me to take them on our trip.

Someone knocked on my door.

I sat down the bagel I was eating and walked to answer it.

The knock came again more urgently.

I opened the door. Standing there was Mr. Boweiler. The fifty-three year old was shifting frantically in place.

"Do you mind?" he asked.

"This is the last time," I said as I opened the door all the way, "I'll be gone for a while on vacation."

He darted past me and headed to my bathroom.

176

Boweiler was one of the first people I met when I moved into the condo. His son had a habit of clogging up their toilet. This was now the third time since I had moved in that Boweiler asked to use mine.

"I already called the plumber," a voice shouted from behind my bathroom door.

...

Roland finished the last touches on his Luke Taylor costume. The ink on his two arms was nearly real. The only way to get the ink off of the skin was to blend to special liquids together with water and soak the area for an hour. After that, one needed to take about three showers to complete the transformation.

After putting on the body suit, Roland felt a burst of confidence. Luke Taylor was one tough looking thug. Roland felt invincible.

A thick, gold chain adorned his neck. Roland placed the voice modulator in it.

"I am one bad ass..." Roland was saying as he burst into laughter. He had forgotten to change the settings on the modulator. He was dressed like Luke but talking like Jenna. Roland recalibrated the modulator to sound deep and somewhat scratchy. That voice fit the Luke character much better.

He opened the drawer of the cosmetic area labeled "Luke Taylor." He took out all the items and placed them in his pockets. In his garage, he went to the Chevy Camaro.

Roland revved it a couple times before leaving.

"A badass car for a badass boy," he said to himself.

...

"Thanks," Boweiler said as he was leaving.

"It's no problem," I said.

The phone rang. I went to get it.

"I really do owe you," he said as he left and closed the door behind him.

"Hello?" I answered the phone.

"You ordered a cab," the voice said with a New Jersey accent.

"Yeah"

"I'm outside waiting."

"Be there in a sec," I said hanging up the phone.

...

Roland was so excited with the idea of killing the traitor that he was speeding. Two cars behind him, a police officer turned on his lights and sped up. Roland pulled over, and the police car stopped behind him.

The officer cautiously approached the Camaro.

"License and registration, sir."

"What did I do?" Luke Taylor asked unaware of the speed he had been going.

"Well, you were doing 65 in a 45 zone"

"Oh," Luke said as he got in his wallet and retrieved the necessary paperwork.

Luke handed his license and registration to the officer. The officer walked back to his car with its lights still flashing to run the identifications.

Those better be worth the price I paid, Roland thought to himself. The falsely constructed record in the file associated with Luke Taylor showed an individual who had two prior traffic citations and an assault on his record. Roland had requested those to aid in the construction of the persona he desired. The characters he took on couldn't be perfect, law abiding citizens. They needed depth.

"Here you go, sir," the officer said handing back the identification along with a speeding ticket, "Watch your speed."

...

I grabbed my things and had just turned to the door when another knock came. Setting them down, I answered the door.

"Sorry to bother you again," Boweiler said, "but my wife asked me to come here and give you this." He held out a twenty dollar bill.

"No, it's fine," I replied not taking the bill from his hand.

"My wife will be upset if you don't take it, so if you see her will you tell her I gave it to you."

"Okay"

"Good, now I have some more cash to take to the strip club when I go," he said with a smile.

"Do you want a hand with that?" he asked gesturing toward the items on the couch.

"Sure, I have a taxi waiting now."

Boweiler and I took all my stuff down to the taxi. It was a van. I had requested a van because I was unsure how much I was going to take with me, and I wanted to be safe rather than sorry.

Sliding the van door close, I told the driver to take me to the rental car place a few miles away. A subcompact was already reserved with my name that would carry me on my journey. I planned to travel as much as Malachi Constant even though I never left the Earth's surface.

...

Boweiler stayed on the curb and observed me leave. In fact, for some reason, he decided to wait there and watch until he lost sight of the van when it turned left two blocks away. He turned and headed back to the condo.

Boweiler was daydreaming about the next lap dance he would get from his favorite stripper, Destiny. He bumped into someone.

"Sorry," he said sincerely.

"Watch where you're going, old man," came a voice that was deep and scratchy.

The old man examined the large figure before him. Tattoos of dragons and skulls covered his arms. His eyes seemed haunted and hateful.

"Yes, sir," Boweiler said submissively.

FOURTEEN

Luke Taylor went to the address he had for the traitor. He knocked. No one answered. Taylor headed back to his car to get the lockpicking gun that he had purchased discretely. Getting the lockpicking device, he placed it in his pocket and headed back to the door that he wanted to get into. Maybe the traitor was asleep, he thought.

Roland had practiced with the tool before. He had become quite adept at quickly picking a standard lock. Before using his device, Roland looked both ways. The coast was clear. He slid it out of his pocket, stood close to the door, and thirty seconds later both the doorknob lock and the deadbolt were picked. Roland smiled. He enjoyed this blue collar criminal activity.

Roland entered the condo and locked the door behind him. It was fairly messy. Empty boxes sat throughout the living room. He pulled the .45 from the holster in the small of his back. As he searched the condo, he found that the traitor was not home. Roland rummaged through some of the items that lay in open sight. A student loan bill, two holiday cards, and a cellphone bill sat on the kitchen table. Roland memorized the number on the cellphone bill. It may come in handy.

How long before the traitor returned to his home? Roland thought. Making himself comfortable on the couch, he placed the gun under one of the decorative pillows. He would wait and surprise the traitor when he came in the door.

...

The police had made headway in the case of Juan Jackson's death. The Tyler Greene tip had been fruitful. They had located the address of Greene in Texas and had obtained a warrant to search the premises.

Local police knocked on the door, but no one was home. Given the nature of the crime that they were investigating, they let themselves in. Searching the premises, the officers found an empty home. No furniture, no mail, no clothes were in the place. It appeared as if the person who lived there had moved. The local police contacted the detectives in charge of the Jackson murder and told them what they had found.

One of the detectives working the case began researching Tyler Greene more thoroughly. He was going to try to locate where this murderer had moved. The other detective had a hunch. She thought that Greene may be an alias. An alias was a fake name used by someone. It was a lie. Like you, I hate being lied to.

The female detective started tracing the money trail. Someone had to have purchased that home. There was no mortgage on record, so the party had to have paid cash. That was a significant amount of money to drop on a place and then simply walk away from.

...

Roland sat on the couch waiting for the traitor to walk in. He constantly fantasized about the moment that the hetero ally who hearted equality would realize his impending demise. Only about a half hour had passed, but Roland was not accustom to waiting for people. He decided he should leave and come back later. Roland could surprise the traitor later tonight.

...

The taxi arrived at the rental car location. I tipped the driver and headed to get my car. Walking inside, I saw a short male with a goatee and a chubby female with red streaks in her hair standing behind the counter.

"Do you have a reservation?" the short male questioned.

I nodded.

"Ok, step over here, I will do your paperwork and get you on your way," he asserted.

I followed his directions.

"License and reservation number," he requested.

I handed him both and waited to get the keys to the subcompact that I had reserved.

"Wow, you're tall," the man at the counter said, looking at my license rather than me.

"Not really," I replied.

The company had found that if its agents noted the size of the person in a complimentary way, it was more likely to get people to upgrade their reservation choice. It had increased the company's profits in the short time that it had been implemented. People liked to feel tall. Men liked to feel big, in a good way. Women like to be told they had long legs. All renters got a compliment that they enjoyed, and the company got more money. Everyone gained. And so on.

...

In fact, I *was* a little taller than average, but I was no giant. As he filled out the appropriate forms, I enjoyed the nostalgia his comment elicited. When I was 16 and got my first license, I was only four foot, eleven inches tall. I was a late bloomer, as they say. Being so short, I couldn't see over the steering wheel of my first car. When I drove, I had to look in the little section available to me *below* the top curvature of the steering wheel but *above* the dashboard. My brother often remarked that it looked like the car didn't have a driver because the door panel was higher than me. So, from the outside looking in, no one that I passed could see a driver.

...

But to continue:

"Here, you go," the rental car agent said, "Are you sure you don't want to upgrade to a larger vehicle?"

I took him up on his suggestion and splurged. This vacation was a long time in the making, and I was going to enjoy it. Placing my luggage and other items in the large trunk, I left the car lot in a luxury sedan. This was going to be a much deserved break, I thought. I hit the highway and headed west.

...

Roland tucked the gun back into the holster in the small of his back and headed out the door. In the hallway, the older man whom he had bumped on the street saw him exiting the condo.

Boweiler asked if he was a friend of the resident.

"No, I'm his brother," Roland stated. It was a lie. Like you, I hate being lied to.

"Oh, nice to meet you, Matt," Boweiler stated sincerely.

Boweiler continued, "I thought he was going to see you in a few days in Los Angeles."

"I had some business to take care of in New York, so I drove up to surprise him. I didn't know he was leaving already," Roland said.

"You just missed him," Boweiler remarked, "he's heading to…"

"The airport," Roland interrupted.

"No, no," Boweiler went on, "the car rental place. He's driving cross country."

Roland attempted to recover, "He must have changed up the plans, last I knew he was going to fly in." He shook his head.

"You never know with that brother of mine," Roland added with a smile, "guess I need to get back to Los Angeles."

Roland left, got in his Camaro, and head back to his place.

Boweiler felt suspicious. His neighbor had never described his brother as big and tattooed. Boweiler headed to his condo to call his neighbor on his cellphone.

"Honey, is that you?" Boweiler's wife proclaimed as he entered his place.

"Yeah"

"Be a dear and run down the street for some milk, eggs, and spaghetti sauce, would you?"

"Okay," Boweiler agreed. He would call when he got back.

...

I headed to Philadelphia. There was a ticket in my luggage to a major sporting event that would be played tomorrow by a team I was a fan of. I had not seen them play for some time, and it would be the first scheduled event on my vacation. I had reserved a room at a hotel within walking distance of the stadium.

Although I had brought some music to listen to on my long trip, I decided to turn on the radio. Seamstress Quick was singing yet another of her heartbreak songs. She had 27 number one hits. All of them were about break ups and the lack in her past significant others. We are Not Getting Back Together Ever, You're a Dork, I'd Rather Kiss a Frog, You have Small Feet, and She is No Me were some of the titles. How many times did she have to lose in a relationship with someone before realizing that maybe it wasn't him it was her? I thought. Regardless, I hopped onto Interstate 90 and sang along.

...

The next song on the radio was a thrash metal song. Kill, kill, kill, destroy, burn to the ground is all the lyrics repeated. It was an odd mix of music but radio was fighting for an audience that was fickle and diverse. The lyrics reminded me of the death of JJ. I pulled the car over to the shoulder and got out my cellphone. Unsure if I was permitted to leave since I was a witness to the murder, I called the police. The detective's number was preprogrammed in my phone. People rarely remembered anyone's phone number by heart. Technology had solved our need to use our memory.

The female detective answered and informed me that I was free to take my vacation. They had my phone number and would call if they had any questions.

"Given new developments," she said, "you are no longer a suspect."

I hadn't been aware that I was a suspect. Wasn't I just a witness? I thought.

"Oh, okay," I replied, "call me, if you think I can help."

I hung up. Well, I didn't really hang up. It was an expression that had stuck around from the early phones that literally had to be rehung in order to disconnect the call. I really just ended the connection with the detective.

Having severed the connection, I jumped back onto the freeway.

...

Boweiler had returned from his errand for his wife. After being reprimanded for getting 2% milk rather than whole milk, he dismissed himself and went to the bed room to call his neighbor. Maybe he was just being feeble-minded, he thought, but why didn't the brother call his neighbor?

The number Boweiler needed was not preprogrammed into his phone, but his neighbor had written it down a couple of days ago. Boweiler looked in the top drawer of the night stand. The paper with the number was missing.

"Honey," he shouted to his wife, "where is the phone number that was in the nightstand?"

"In your phone, silly," she came back, "I put it in yesterday. No use keeping scraps of paper around."

Boweiler had not thought to look for it in his phone. He found it and called. It rang twice, and, then, the voicemail kicked on. Boweiler decided to try later. He didn't want to explain his suspicions over voicemail.

...

The lead detective on JJ's case uncovered tenuous evidence that there could be a link between Tyler Greene and Kevin Roland. She dug deeper hoping to find something more solid. As it was, it would not be enough to get a warrant to search any of the numerous properties held by Kevin Roland. She considered telling the other detective about it, but she didn't want him to dismiss it outright. He was always critical of her ideas. She could, she thought, always pay Mr. Roland a visit and just have a chat. For now, she disregarded the idea. She needed to find something more substantial.

...

Roland got home and called one of his many contacts. He needed information on the traitor's scheduled vacation. Roland had a shady private investigator who could find just about anyone. He called him, told him what he needed, and said there would be a nice bonus if it was delivered soon. The private investigator had so many gambling debts, he jumped at the opportunity to make some more cash and keep the bookies off his back a little longer.

...

The female detective decided to take her lead and treat it is as if it was a fact. Tyler Greene was Kevin Roland. Now, she needed to only find a way to prove it. With some technical assistance, she may just be able to do that. She headed to the tech department to find her friend who could analyze audio and find matches.

She would have the technician compare audioclips of Tyler Greene saying "sorry" while he was at the rally to other clips of Roland when he announced that he would purchase the Queen of the Prairies conglomerate. The technician informed the detective that he had more pressing matters, but he assured her that he would have the comparison done before the end of the day.

...

Roland's phone rang. It was the private investigator.

"I got some news, and some feelers out to get more info, you ready?"

"Yeah, let me get to my desk." Roland wanted to write down every detail, so he could plan his next move.

"Okay, whatcha got?"

"Well, before I tell you anything," the voice dictated, "let's talk pay."

Roland was frustrated by this inconvenience. The other on the phone was gambling that Roland really wanted in the information. The private investigator liked to gamble, and he did it now.

"I'll give you one piece of his itinerary at the normal rate. The second will cost you an additional 10%. Each after that goes up 10% more."

"Now listen here," Roland began, but he stopped himself. It would take him days to locate a person if he didn't have access to the shady private investigator's network.

"Okay, but it better be worth it."

The voice on the other end of the line told Roland that the person he sought would end his cross country trip in Los Angeles. He gave Roland the hotel name, address, and even the room number that was reserved. Roland smiled.

"He is not set to check in for another 11 days," the voice added.

"Well, where will he be between now and then?"

"Driving there," the voice said dryly.

"No shit, but it doesn't take 11 days to get there," Roland exclaimed.

The private investigator told Roland that he could give him more information about the early part of the guy's trip when some of his contacts got back to him.

"I know he has a sister in Chicago, a Father in St. Louis, a high school friend in the Kansas City area, an aunt in DC, and a hotel reserved in Vegas," the voice listed, "Oh, and a brother in Los Angeles." Roland already knew about the brother. He had recently learned about him by talking to the traitor's neighbor.

"So, is he driving straight to Chicago? Or St. Louis? Or what?" Roland asked.

"I don't know," said the contact, "I have people who still need to report back to me."

Roland told him to call as soon as he knew more about the schedule.

"Oh," said the private investigator, "I have another piece of information for you, but it is *really* gonna cost you." Roland could tell that whatever it was, it was good. He could hear the private investigator's giddiness over the phone. The private investigator told Roland it would cost five times the usual amount. Roland's curiosity was too great to refuse the cost. "The police are beginning to suspect that you are linked to the recent murder of Juan Jackson," the voice said.

...

The male detective on the Jackson case came into the female's office.

"I've got a lead," he stated.

"Really? What is it?" she said. She hoped he would mention Kevin Roland so that she could share the work she had been putting together.

"I have confirmation that Leonard Debs was at the rally the day before the poisoning."

Debs was a convict who ran a small gang. He had done a number of hits in the past, but police could never gain enough on him to convict him.

"So?" she asked.

"Juan Jackson, as the public defender, had taken Debs' case when police found enough to convict him on drug trafficking. Jackson had promised to get Debs off, but he failed to do so. Not until Debs served time did he locate a high end attorney. It appears Debs paid the attorney with laundered money from his drug sales. Another inmate turned informant told us that Debs mentioned, on numerous occasions, that he was going to make his lawyer pay for the time he got stuck behind bars," the male detective answered. "But as a public defender, there are probably tons of ex-cons who had a vendetta against Jackson," the female detective pointed out. The male detective told her that there was a ton of circumstantial evidence. Debs had knee surgery three months ago and had crutches, owned the same brand and style of sunglasses, was at the rally on the first day, probably doing recon, and was about the same build as Tyler Greene.

"I guess we can look into it," she said, but she wasn't convinced they were taking the investigation in the right direction. Her and her male colleague headed out of the office to track down Debs for questioning.

...

Roland was nervous about the last bit of information he got from his contact. He would need to investigate and find out what the police knew. Roland was pretty sure that he had left no traces for the police to follow, but he needed to be certain. Tomorrow, he would contact the officer in the department that he had bribed before and have the young man dig around to see what the police knew.

For now, however, Roland wanted to start planning his next move. Where would he meet up with the rabid traitor? If he could find where the traveler was going before Chicago, Roland surmised that he could kill him before the traitor got a chance to see his family one last time. Otherwise, Roland contemplated, he would need to catch the traitor in Vegas to limit the chance of friends and family that may be in the way.

...

After driving a few hours, I reached the outskirts of Philadelphia. A sign made certain I knew what the city's name meant. It looked like this:

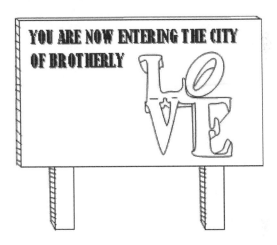

Next to the sign stood an older, homeless man with a grey, shaggy beard. He flipped off the passing cars with a smile. The homeless guy had nothing better to do than enjoy the irony.

I got to my hotel earlier than expected. Traffic in the New York area was lighter than anticipated. It was still awful, but it was not as horrid as I had thought it would be.

After placing my things in my hotel room, I went and asked the desk worker if there was a good place to eat within walking distance. I had had such a light lunch that my stomach was rumbling. The boyish-looking young man told me the directions to a place that he described as "quirky, but good." I headed to find this quirky place.

···

I followed the directions provided to me by the hotel worker. A sign informed me that I had arrived at the Goodbye Blue Monday Cafe. It looked like this:

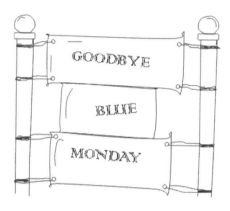

To make sure people knew that it was a restaurant, another sign stated that it was a place to eat. It looked like this:

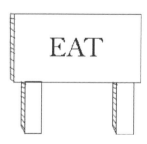

I entered the establishment. A small chalkboard display in the lobby had the words "Seat Yourself" written on it. I passed it and sought a table. The place was fairly crowded. I almost sat at a table with disproportional stripes on it. The top of it looked like this:

In the poorly lit restaurant, I hadn't noticed the mess on it. I got up and looked for another table. Across the room, I found a table with three, equal sized stripes on its top. It looked like this:

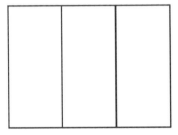

It was clean. As sat down, I heard a commotion to my left. I turned and looked. The party to my left was celebrating someone's birthday.

"Happy Birthday, Wanda June," a middle-aged woman was announcing to an older lady.

"Oh, Penelope, you shouldn't have," the older lady replied modestly.

I scanned the crowd around Wanda June. Many of them looked as if they could be related. I assumed it was a birthday party for their mother or grandmother. One table to the party's left appeared to have been reserved for others who were coming to this celebration. It looked like this:

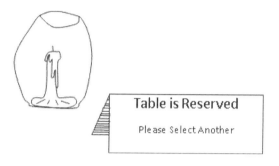

I stopped watching and turned in my chair to peruse the menu. A Philly Cheesesteak caught my eye. How could I go to Philadelphia and not have one? I thought. A big breasted waitress came to my table.

"Do you know what you want?" she asked.

Looking up from my menu, I saw her. She was wearing a tight t-shirt that seemed to be painted onto her curve form. I paused and read the shirt. It looked like this:

The dim light along with the curvature of the letters caused by her bosom made it hard to read the text on the shirt. I stared trying to make out the words.

"You're reading my shirt, I know," she said sarcastically. She assumed I was staring at her breasts.

"Yeah," I said not thinking.

"Do you know what you want?" she repeated.

I told her that I'd have the Philly Cheesesteak and a beer. She told me it would be right out.

...

The birthday party for Wanda June was laughing and having a gay old time.

As I waited for my food, I scanned the walls. They were covered with pictures, awards, and odd artifacts. Many of the things hanging there I couldn't make out. The restaurant should have hung more lights. I looked at the wall nearest to my table. On it was a plaque that looked like this:

...

My big breasted waitress returned with my sandwich and beer. She sat down the plate and beer on the table. Then, she reached in her apron and pulled out a smiley face button.

"Goodbye Blue Monday," she said in a cheerful but seemingly automated way.

"Huh?"

"With every order, you get a smiley button," she replied. I only shook my head as she left. I picked up the pin. It looked like this:

I took a bite of my sandwich. It was delicious. I was hungry and started to devour it. About half way through my sandwich, the Wanda June's birthday party was up and getting ready to leave. I took another bite. It hit me. Another thought bubble exploded in my psyche.

This bubble was different. I didn't shake but got extremely nauseous. The Philly Cheesesteak was about to come back up. I stood up quickly in an attempt to get to the bathroom but didn't realize I didn't have time. My vomit propelled out and onto Wanda June and Penelope. I was pretty sure that wasn't what she had wished for when she blew out the candles earlier.

FIFTEEN

Well, I didn't have to throw up anymore. The nausea passed, but the shakes came. I needed to write. The urge was painful. Tears came sliding down my cheek as I wiped a mixture of gastric acid, saliva, and a chunk of cheesesteak from my chin. Without asking for permission, I reached into the apron of my waitress, who had come over to see if everything was alright, and grabbed her ink pen. I turned back to my table, flipped over the paper place mat, and began to write. The first sentence read:

In his Manhattan home, Vonnegut had chuckled when they told him his name was 124C.

"Are you alright?" the waitress asked sincerely.

"Yeah," I replied, "sorry about the mess."

"Must be a stomach virus," I added. It was a lie. Like you, I hate being lied to.

...

Roland decided that the best plan of action was to go to Vegas. The strategy not only allowed him to sit in waiting to spring on the traitor as well as get away from potential police questioning but it also gave him a playground for passing the days until the traitor arrived. He called his private investigator contact and confirmed the traitor's hotel reservation dates. Then, he called and made travel arrangements. He would arrive in Vegas a week before the traitor and stay in the same upscale hotel on the strip. Calling his private jet carrier, Roland instructed them to make the plane ready. He would pack the Luke Taylor costume as well as the Paul Venter costume as to give him some flexibility in disguises. Roland would also take the .45 and a few boxes of ammo. Owning his own plane meant he didn't need to go through security.

...

Leonard Debs answered his door. Two police detectives asked to speak with him. Knowing that the drugs that had been in his home yesterday were already shipped, Debs wasn't worried about them searching his home. He welcomed them in. Debs was slightly nervous. Cops always meant future trouble. He'd never had an interview with them and not been brought up on some charge in the near future.

A male and a female detective asked him questions about the rally that he had attended. Which days was he there? Why did he go? Did he see Juan Jackson there? Did he go alone? Did he leave with anyone? Which side of the street did he stay on most?

The police already knew the answers to most of the questions because of the surveillance footage that they had analyzed. They needed to know if Debs would answer honestly. He did.

"We heard you had surgery a while back and were on crutches for a while, is that right?" the male officer probed.

Debs told them that he had needed orthoscopic surgery to repair his left knee. Coincidentally, it was the same leg that Tyler Greene had a cast on.

"Do you still have the crutches?" the female officer queried.

"Yeah," Debs answered, "I think they are in the closet."

"Can we see them?" the male officer asked.

"Sure"

Debs went to the other room and brought to crutches back with him. The two officers inspected every inch of the two crutches. An inch was a unit of distance. It broke into smaller units, and one could see the size of an inch on a ruler. It looked like this:

Satisfied that the two crutches were normal, the officers handed them back to Debs. They asked him a few other questions about the second day of the rally. Did he go to the rally on the second day? If not, what did he do? Where was he? Could he show any proof of where he was?

Debs answered all the questions. The police officers felt content with his responses.

"We may be back to see you again soon," the male detective said as they left.

•••

Roland headed to his private plane with multiple bags. He planned to be gone for no more than two weeks, but with two different identities other than his own, there was much he needed to bring. The .45, lockpicking tool, two knives, rope, brass knuckles, and assortment of other items filled one duffle bag.

He had been thinking about his situation. The worse case that he could conceive was that the cops determined that he had poisoned the guy with the ugly neck scar. If that happened, he would leave the country immediately. There were numerous countries who did not allow for extradition to the United States. Most were in places with people Roland could not stand to live near. Asians, Arabs, and Blacks were the most common groups in such countries. Other countries on the list were dangerous or currently considered a war zone. The only two that had White people that he would consider moving to were Bosnia and Serbia. Roland had called his realtor and told him to lock down a vacation home in Sarajevo.

On his way to his awaiting jet, Roland ran to one of his banks. He had called ahead because he was going to make a large withdrawal as well as transfer funds. Roland had $20 million transferred to an untouchable, Swiss account. The Swiss account already had a $10 million in it, but Roland wanted to make sure he was comfortable if he had to live somewhere else. Thirty million would go far in a place like Bosnia. He also took three briefcases with digital locks to the bank and withdrew $5 million dollars.

Following Roland through the lobby with two armed guards, the bank manager asked if Roland felt the bank had not provided adequate services. As Roland walked out of the bank with three briefcases full of cash, his only reply was, "It's not you, it's me."

Later that night, Roland would be in Vegas staying at the same high end hotel in the middle of the strip that the traitor had reserved for his vacation.

...

After questioning Debs, the detectives arrived back at the station. The female officer headed straight to the technician she had asked a favor of to see if he had run voice recognition software to compare Tyler Greene's vocal patterns to Kevin Roland's. The technician informed her that he had put that on the back burner due to other more pressing assignments. He didn't want his supervisor writing him up again. She told him to call her as soon as he knew something. He agreed.

A major break in the case would come in a few days, but it would have nothing to do with the technician's work.

...

I paid my bill at the Goodbye Blue Monday Café and headed back to the hotel. The game was tomorrow, and I wanted to get a good night's rest.

When I got back to my room, I didn't call the front desk for a wake up call. I was going to sleep in. Being on vacation, I could think of no reason to get up early. In fact, the game that I had tickets for was not until the afternoon, so I would likely sleep in until the late morning hours.

I lay on the bed and fell fast to sleep. After a few hours, I awoke from a nightmare. I was huddled in the closet. Sleepwalking was an act I had never done before. Then again, I had never pissed myself in public or vomited on two complete strangers either. I trembled as I recalled my dream. In the dream, a tattooed man with hate in his eyes shot me through a closet door. What the hell was going on with me? I knew there was no easy answer but to simply endure it and hope it passed.

...

I awoke late in the morning and felt fairly refreshed. The residue of the dream still disturbed my mind, but I tried to not think about. I checked out of the hotel, packed the rental car with my belongings, and walked to the game.

My team lost, but I enjoyed getting to watch them play. I left the game, got in the car, and began my eleven hour road trip to see my sister in Chicago.

As I pulled out of the parking garage, a truck nearly hit me. The driver was texting and not paying attention to the road. The truck was an Ajax truck and looked like this:

I drove for a while and realized I needed gas. The luxury car didn't seem to get very good gas mileage. While filling up, I grabbed some snacks for the road and some chocolate. My niece loved chocolate, but my sister would never let her have any. I was going to be the "bad Uncle" and give it to her as a gift along with a teddy bear that was in my luggage.

Leaving the gas station, I hopped on Interstate 76 and headed west. Along the way, someone had spent a ton on advertising their tourist trap. The first sign was only a few miles down where I entered the highway. It read:

VISIT SACRED MIRACLE
CAVE

162 MILES

Less than two hours down the road, I was reminded of the "Miracle Cave." The billboard read:

VISIT SACRED MIRACLE
CAVE

52 MILES

What the hell was a sacred miracle cave anyway? Their advertising was making a dent on my decision-making. I was considering going to it just to see what it was. Did some stigmata appear there or something? I thought. I turned the radio on to pass the time. Seamstress Quick was singing of heartbreak. She had been dumped, *again*. I sang along.

In forty minutes flat, I saw the next sign for the cave. The sign was the largest of the bunch and was made of neon so that it would not be missed at night. It read:

VISIT SACRED
MIRACLE CAVE

Under the sign was another one that read "Access the Prophets" and had pictures of four men. The first was labeled Abraham. The second labeled Jesus. And the last was labeled Zoroaster. The third one in line had no name. Since the other prophets appeared in alphabetical order, I assumed it was suppose to be Mohammed. The cave owner probably didn't want some crazy jihadist blowing up their precious, sacred cave.

I almost exited the highway to check out this strange cave, but I knew I couldn't. It was still quite a long trip to get to Chicago, and my sister would be up into the wee hours of the morning waiting for my arrival. I was making good time and needed to keep it that way.

One exit further down the freeway there was yet another billboard. Whoever was running that cave sure was persistent. The sign read:

I hit the gas. No turning back for me. I had family to see.

SIXTEEN

Roland landed in Vegas and had a limousine waiting to take him to his hotel. On the flight, he had planned out his week. First, he would relax and gamble. When the week was coming to an end and the traitor was about to arrive, he would bribe a maid to get a master key to the traitor's room. Maids were so underpaid that one would likely jump at the chance to make the cash. He would then go to the room and await the traitor. Roland smiled thinking about the look on that pathetic traitor's face.

...

Listen:

I was finished driving across the state of Pennsylvania and entered the outskirts of Cleveland. There was a large traffic jam on the interstate. Some teenaged girl had been texting and caused a massive pile up. It had been twenty minutes, and I hadn't moved a foot. I called my sister to tell her that I would be later than expected. As the phone rang, I hoped my niece would not be asleep already. My sister assured me that she would stay up until I arrived regardless of how late in the night or early in the morning it was.

After another twenty minutes, the traffic had moved enough that I could reach the next exit. I decided to jump off the freeway and find a way around this mess. Not knowing the area and leaving my GPS in the glove box, I attempted to stay on streets that were close to the highway.

Bars on shop windows, graffiti, and boarded up homes suggested this was not the best of neighborhoods. I went over some railroad tracks. The luxury car had such remarkable suspension that I barely felt the bump. To my right, I noticed what appeared to be an abandoned warehouse. Backed into one of the docks was a truck with the word "Acme" on it. It looked like this:

Down the street, I saw a family on the side of the otherwise barren road. They looked stranded. A middle-aged man and woman were accompanied by three small kids. It is getting late, I thought, and those kids should probably not be out in this sort of neighborhood. I pulled over to see if I could help them.

As I got out of my car, the man quickly approached. He looked blue. Not the color but the feeling. If I could see his thoughts, they would have likely looked like this:

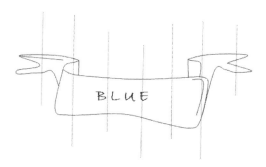

The man looked as if he would break into tears at any moment. I was unsure if it was the situation that caused it or that a stranger finally stopped.

"What's wrong?" I asked.

"Yo no hablo Inglés," he said frustrated as if he had told other good Samaritans the same but with no avail. Lucky for him, I spoke Spanish. He let me know that something was wrong with his car and thought it was the transmission. Every time he called a tow truck company, he found that no one understood him. I told him I would translate for him. He gave a heartfelt smile and thanked me. We called the tow truck company and told them the location.

As we waited, we chatted. I saw a bracelet on his left wrist. It looked like this:

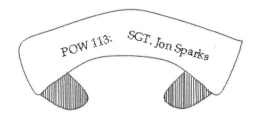

I asked him what the bracelet was. He told me that it noted that his brother-in-law had been a POW in one of the many wars from America's past. America was good at war. Since its founding in 1776, the United States had been in some sort of war or conflict for 216 out of 237 years. In fact, the only time the US could make it for a five year period was from 1935 to 1940. Part of the reason it kept its nose clean then was the Great Depression and isolationism. Nowadays, war had become so commonplace that some Americans took it as the norm. They didn't long for the soldiers to return home and did not keep vigils in hopes of an end to violence. For many, they just went on with their lives as if nothing significant was occurring. "Just go out and shop" was the motto.

The tow truck showed up. I translated everything necessary to get the driver to take the car to a nearby shop. Being unsure if the family would need a translator later in the night, I gave the man with the bracelet my cellphone number and told him he could call if needed. He thanked me profusely and offered me money. I told him that I could not accept his money and asked that he made sure to stop the next time he saw someone stranded. He promised he would.

I got back in my car, drove through Cleveland, and jumped back on the interstate. Interstate 90 would take me the rest of the way to Chicago. I hopped on it and hit the gas in the hopes of making up some lost time.

···

Roland got to his penthouse suite in the luxurious hotel. A doorman had the remainder of his items. Roland tipped the doorman and closed the door behind him. The suite was spacious and extravagant. Opulence had no better home than Las Vegas. The suite had multiple rooms, marble everywhere, and a private pool. Before placing the three briefcases filled with cash into the digital safe of the room, Roland took out one hundred thousand dollars. That should be enough for some fun tonight, he thought.

As a billionaire, he would draw attention. Roland decided to change into a character. Luke Taylor was out. Taylor did not look like he would have the kind of money Roland was about to throw around. It would look more like a bank robber trying to double his earnings. Roland decided to take on the Paul Venter persona. Venter was simple enough. Some colored contacts, a wig, fake nose, a cheap suit, and a bushy moustache would come across as a tacky, but wealthy, business owner.

As Venter, Roland began his gambling at the roulette wheel. He never bet on black. Red was bad enough in his mind. Most times, he simply bet even or odd. Venter left the roulette table with an extra ten thousand. He saw an attractive blonde in a black cocktail dress sitting at the high stakes blackjack table. Venturing over, he sat next to her.

"Any luck?" he asked, his voice modulated by the small, discrete necklace he wore.

"It comes and goes," she responded.

He pulled out a wad of cash to make sure she saw his wealth and asked the dealer for twenty thousand in chips.

"It's a $5000 table," the dealer announced in a questioning way as to see if the gentleman wanted more chips.

"That's fine," Venter replied, "I feel lucky."

Venter was lucky. He not only flirted and seduced the young beauty to come to his room later but turned his twenty thousand into another hundred thousand. The blonde and Venter were having a gay old time. Laughing and flirting and enjoying passing glances at each other, they garnered a comment from a Texas oil man playing at the table.

"Why don't you two just get a room already?" he proffered.

"I already have one, the penthouse," Venter replied smugly.

"Oh, really?" the blonde said excitedly, "I've never seen the penthouse."

They finished their hands. Both lost that time. And they headed for the young beauty to see a penthouse.

...

As I reached Gary, Indiana, I pulled over to the shoulder of the highway to send my sister a quick message. I was tired, but I didn't have much further to go. She replied that she was tired but still waiting up.

...

Taking the private elevator to his penthouse, Roland escorted the blonde to his suite. This is gonna create a problem, the blonde thought. She had planned to drug him with ruffies and steal whatever she could find in his possession. Ruffies were known as the date rape drug. The drug was a strong depressant that would knock out anyone who took too much of it. The blonde didn't plan to rape him. At least not physically. She would, however, take everything he physically had. Her problem was that she usually had backup. They were in the lobby awaiting her call with the room number. Unfortunately, they would not be able to access the penthouse given the private elevator.

The blonde was a career criminal. She had used her looks to do a variety of crimes. From being a distraction in a robbery to prostitution, she had preyed on the wealthy. Most never reported the crime. The victims were too embarrassed by the outcomes and had public images to maintain.

Closing the door behind them, Roland asked, "So, what's your name?"

"Ashley," the blonde said. It was lie. She never gave her real name to anyone. Like you, I hate being lied to.

"And your's?" she added with a playful smile.

"Paul," Roland said. It was lie too. Lying about their identity and doing blue collar crime was all the two really had in common. Like you, I hate being lied to.

Roland showed Ashley around the penthouse. They stepped outside the large glass doors to the back patio. A pool with crystal blue water was lit.

"Wanna take a dip?" Roland suggested.

"Nah, that seems so cliché," Ashley responded, "I like excitement." She was rubbing his arm. Ashley knew she had to heighten his sexual desire so that he became more vulnerable.

They walked back inside.

"I want to experience a man who can demonstrate just how crazy he is," Ashley reported.

"He has to let me feel like he has nothing to loose. Most wealthy men can't do that. You're not boring like all those others, are you?"

Roland didn't answer.

"So, what do you want me to do to show I'm a little crazy?" he asked.

"Well, if I have to tell you, then you must not be that crazy," she playfully whispered in his ear as she ran her fingers through it.

Roland was turned on and nervous at the same time. What if she realizes it is a wig? He thought. Roland stepped away slowly in an attempt to keep her from touching his fake hair and to reestablish some sense of power.

"Okay, I have an idea, go sit at the table," he commanded.

Roland brought over a deck of cards, three shot glasses, and a bottle of expensive whiskey. He told her they would play a version of strip poker. The rules would be straightforward. The losing player of each hand would either forfeit their money, drink three shots of whiskey, or take off one item of clothes. Ashley thought the game was perfect. She didn't mind taking off her clothes and the drinks on the table gave her the potential to ruffie this loser. If she won and he gave up his cash, she was getting what she came for anyway. In Roland's mind, it was a winning situation, too. He would either get her drunk and take advantage of her or give her money that he didn't really need.

"It's a start," she said playfully.

They began playing with a five hundred dollar ante. After three hands, Ashley was missing two shoes, and Roland was missing three thousand dollars. Both thought it was going well. Five hands later, Roland was down another thousand dollars, but Ashley had removed her two thigh highs and had selected to reach under her cocktail dress and take her G-string off. She was hoping that move would distract him more. Ashley felt that she needed to change up the game in some way.

Ashley got up from her chair and walked over the wealthy man. She pulled his chair back and, then, straddled him. Pressed against him, she could feel that he was excited.

"We need to raise the stakes," she whispered seductively in his ear.

"I believe you're holding back and need to be a little more crazy," she added.

In the voice of Paul Venter, Roland replied, "I am up for anything." He was. Roland hadn't been with a woman for a while, and this blonde was a mixture of a supermodel and a porn star.

"You get crazy enough," the woman whispered, "and I'll call my twin over for some *real* fun." It was not quite a lie, but it did conceal an important truth. Her twin was male.

Ashley went to her purse and took out a bag of cocaine. She told him that they would raise the stakes. The ante would jump to five thousand. If she won, he would do a line of cocaine and give up the cash. If he won, she would lose the money and give him oral pleasure. Roland didn't mind the cocaine. He had done numerous drugs in the early stages of his wealth in search of meaning. Roland was on a role and figured he would be getting pleased rather than snorting any of it anyway. He agreed to her terms.

Roland ended up with a fullhouse, aces over eights.

Before showing his cards, he decided he should up the stakes again.

"Let's be crazy," he told her, "if I win, you call your twin and we have some fun, if you win, I'll do three lines of coke."

Ashley only smiled and agreed. If she lost, she would just call her twin in the lobby and have him ruff up this schmuck, so they could steal his things.

Roland got excited. He laid his cards on the table triumphantly.

"Oh, no wonder, you wanted to raise the stakes," Ashley said jokingly.

"So, you're gonna call her," Roland said excitedly.

"Not quite"

Ashley laid her hand on the table. She had four of a kind. Wanting to call her twin and get this drama over with so she could find another victim, she had attempted to throw the game. Ashley had kept only a seven and a two but had drawn three more sevens. Sticking to his word, Roland snorted the three lines of coke. A rush overtook him. His heart was racing, and he felt invincible.

He shook his head and rubbed his nostrils. The cocaine made him crazy. "Let's up the stakes," he shouted, not aware of how loud he was speaking. Ashley agreed.

"You want crazy, you want crazy," he kept repeating as he walked to the other side of the room. "Can you even handle crazy?" he asked. "Oh yeah," she came back in a moaning way as if she was auditioning for a role in porn.

Roland went to the gun case. He removed the special, small, metal covers on the cylinder that aided the gun's suppression. The covers limited the easy rotation of the cylinder. He grabbed the six armor piercing bullets. Turning around with the gun in his hand, Ashley cowered.

"Oh, no," Roland rushed to say, "I'm not going to shoot you."

"Relax, *live* a little," he added as the effects of the cocaine were growing.

As he walked over to her, he opened the gun to show her that it was not loaded. Ashley sighed in relief. Roland set the gun on the table and placed the six bullets next to it.

The coked-out-of-his-mind, wealthy man sat across from the dangerously beautiful blonde. He smiled. He was invincible.

"Simple, we put all our money on the table," he started.

"Whoever looses has to play Russian roulette. We will start with the gun empty and add a bullet ever round. Whoever is still alive in the end keeps all the money."

This was not crazy, it was stupid, Ashley thought. What would he do if she tried to leave? There was a gun now in the drama and that raised the stakes in too many ways.

"I'm not..." Ashley began, but Roland held up a finger to silence her. He walked to the digital safe and withdrew five-hundred thousand dollars more from one of the briefcases. Setting it on the table with all the other cash he had on hand, he smiled sadistically.

"Look, we will play to five bullets, if we get there. If someone can put that gun to their head with five bullets in the six chambers, spin the cylinder, and still not die, they deserve the cash."

Ashley agreed to the terms. She knew that before it got to that point, the crazy person would be dead or she would excuse herself and get the hell out of there. Ashley acted as if she was placing all her cash on the table, but she had tucked ten thousand in her bra when Roland left to get the gun. She had also put ruffies in the whiskey.

Roland dealt the first hand.

...

The lead female detective on the Juan Jackson case awoke from a nightmare. She was sweating profusely. In the dream, Kevin Roland had tied her up. She was suspended in the air. Her arms were tied in opposite directions to the rafters of the warehouse they were in. Her legs were spread and tied to two objects on the floor. The detective was a human X.

"You need to be freed," Kevin Roland had said maliciously.

He took a small hatchet from a table. One swift swing and she was missing her left foot. She screamed in horror and pain. Another equally brutal swing removed her right leg below the knee. Blood was everywhere. She cried out for help, but none came.

Roland got a ladder and moved it close to her. Surgically, he swung the instrument of death and took off her left hand. She felt her consciousness waning as she bled from three appendages and hung nearly lifeless, still suspended by the fourth.

"You are free," Kevin Roland announced as he swung the hatchet at the fourth, and final, appendage. Whack!

She woke. Sitting up in sweat soaked pajamas, she tried to catch her breath. The detective went to her bathroom and splashed cold water on her face. It would be difficult to get back to sleep, but she knew she needed more rest. Tomorrow would be a long day.

As she lay back in bed, she was surer than ever that Kevin Roland had something to do with the death of Juan Jackson. She just needed to find proof.

...

But to continue:

Roland could only manage to get a pair of tens in the first hand. Lucky for him, Ashley had only a pair of sevens.

With a twisted smile, Roland said, "You get the *easy* round."

The gun wasn't loaded, but Ashley was still nervous as she picked it up. She put it to her temple and pulled the trigger. Even without a round in it, she twitched nervously expecting it to go off. Roland could not contain his elation at watching a person potentially kill themselves. He needed to see it again.

"No, no," he said, "that doesn't count, you have to spin the cylinder or it's not really Russian roulette."

"But…" Ashley began.

"I said no," Roland stated forcefully.

"Okay, okay," she withdrew her objection. Picking back up the gun, she spun the cylinder. The hum of the metal spinning was music to Roland's ears. Ashley placed it to her temple again. Click. Roland let out a sign of pleasure.

Ashley's heart was racing. She didn't know if she could go another round. How could she get out of this? If she lost the next round, she considered using the one bullet to take out the prick across that table that had gotten her into this mess. But, she was not a murderer.

Maybe she could take a drink of the ruffied whiskey before putting the gun to her head the next time. It would surely knock her out, and she would be out of the game. He would likely rape her if she did that, but she didn't know if she had a choice. Walking away from this psycho may prove too dangerous.

It was her time to deal, and she worked to help her odds. As she shuffled, she noted the card at the bottom on the deck. If it was useful for her when she saw her hand, she would deal it to herself. It was not much of an advantage, but it was all she could think of in the situation.

•••

I got to my sister's place in the wee hours of the morning, and she was up waiting.

Referencing my niece who was sleeping in the other room, my sister said, "I told her that her Uncle was coming, and she said 'yippie, is he bringing me gifts?'"

I smiled. I had brought some gifts for my only niece. She would be up and well rested in three hours. Excited to see what her uncle had brought, she would wake me. The short nap had not refreshed me as much as I had hoped it would. I had to get some coffee.

My niece's mother frowned as I gave the small girl some chocolate. My sister didn't like her daughter having chocolate. Otherwise, both mother and daughter delighted in the various gifts that I had brought. My sister nearly cried when I gave her the book of poems written by our mother.

•••

Ashley dealt the card and knew that the bottom card was a two of clubs. Great, she thought, why couldn't it be an ace? Maybe her luck was running out.

She looked at her cards. The three, four, and five of clubs sat in her hand with a nine of diamonds and a jack of hearts.

Roland asked for three cards. Ashley had to make a decision. Give the crazy guy the two of clubs when she gave him three cards or keep it for herself. She handed him three cards.

Ashley told the coked-out freak that she would take two cards. She hoped for the best.

"Ok," he said proudly, "the time has come to see what we're made of." What either of them was made of may be lying on the floor next to their dead body in a moment. Their grey matter splashed on the floor like some postmodern artwork. He laid down three kings and smiled.

Ashley laid down a two-through-six straight flush and sighed in relief. She had dodged a bullet literally.

•••

As the female detective in charge of JJ's case was driving into the station and I was playing with my niece and watching cartoon, Roland was about to put a loaded gun to his head and pull the trigger.

•••

But to continue:

Roland grabbed the revolver and opened the cylinder. He took one bullet from the table and slotted it into place. Ashley was uncertain if she should let him go through with it. If he shot himself, she could grab the cash and exit. The noise, however, may bring people, and she would have too much to explain. The gun, the cocaine, all the money, the dead body, their short acquaintanceship yet insane interactions. Maybe she should tell him to take a drink of the whiskey.

"Wait," she interrupted as he cocked the hammer back, "why not take a shot of whiskey for good luck."

"I don't need luck," Roland said arrogantly, "but, for you, why the hell not."

He grabbed the shot glass closest to him and threw it down the hatch. Unfortunately for Ashley, it had the least amount of ruffies in it. In her rush, she had poured most of the powder into the middle glass. The small amount of depressant was no match for the cocaine in his system. Cocaine was a stimulant. Ruffies were a depressant. They were fighting within his blood stream to dominate his mood. The cocaine won by a landslide. It was like a heavyweight boxer taking on a newborn baby.

Roland took the revolver and spun the cylinder. He placed it to his temple. Roland pulled the trigger. Unlike Ashley, he didn't flinch. Click. He set the gun back on the table and smiled deviously.

"Next round," he said and noticed the panic in Ashley's eyes. He reveled in the play on words. A round was a game of poker. It was also the name given to ammunition.

As he began to deal the next hand, he noticed the numerous empty slots in the back of the gun's cylinder.

"Hold up," he said as he lay the cards down.

He picked back up the gun. Ashley feared he was going to shot her dead where she sat. He was insane, she thought, what am I still doing here?

Roland opened the revolver. A round was in the firing slot. That didn't make sense, he thought, I should be dead. He examined the bullet carefully. The round was a dud. It had been poorly manufactured, and its primer was too deep to be hit by the hammer of the gun.

"Oh, my god," Ashley exclaimed realizing what had happened.

"I should go," she added as she got up.

"No, we are not done," Roland stated authoritatively, "sit back down."

"I'm going to go to the bathroom, and you'd better be here when I get back."

Roland got up, grabbed the gun, and pocketed the bullets. She was not going to use it to threaten him to leave or shot him. He would have it to scare her from trying to get out the door.

Still somewhat shaken from the recent events, Roland went to the bathroom and splashed his face with water. While the adhesive for his fake moustache was suppose to be water-resistant, the prop was peeling off the left side of his upper lip. He pushed it down, but it would not remain in place.

Ashley decided she couldn't run away. It was too risky. He now had the gun. Maybe she should seduce him and use her beauty as her last advantage. She grabbed a handful of the cash on the table and threw it in her small purse. Taking off her dress but putting her G-string and thigh highs back on, she awaited his return.

Roland left the bathroom holding the moustache on with his left hand. He rubbed it in an attempt to appear that he was thinking.

He entered the main room to the see the blonde half-naked and bent over the table. She was looking back over her shoulder.

"Isn't this what you really wanted," she asserted.

Roland was confused. He was feeling so horny but the moustache was not the only issue. The fake nose was starting to peel too. What would happen if she found out his real identity?

"I changed my mind," he said sternly, "you need to go."

Ashley didn't need to be told twice. She slipped into her dress quickly, grabbed her purse and shoes, and darted for the door.

"Maybe, I could see you tomorrow night," Roland said. It was too late. She was gone.

...

Casey Eisenstein was a young engineering student at the only university in Ilium. His roommate was working on a report for his class on current events. The roommate's paper addressed the death of the public defender, Juan Jackson.

"Let me read this to you and tell me what you think," Casey's roommate asserted.

Attentively, Casey listened.

"Wait," Casey said, "read that part again."

"According to witnesses," the roommate said, "the criminal used a crutch rigged to inject the toxic poison ricin."

Casey jumped up.

"What's wrong?"

"Nothing. I have to go, *right* now."

Casey had designed the crutch for Kevin Dwayne Roland. Before getting accustomed to changing into various characters, Roland had met face to face with Casey to explain the design he wanted. He had also met Casey to pay for the constructed item. Roland had told Casey the needle in the crutch was to pick up trash with. Being naïve and young, Casey had thought nothing of the silly idea. The young engineer had only seen a way to not only make money but make a connection with a billionaire.

Casey hopped on his motorized scooter and headed straight to the police station. He needed to tell the detectives working the case that he believed he had constructed the crutch. Fearful that he may be charged with some crime like conspiracy, he nonetheless knew that the right thing to do was be transparent. He was unlike most governments in that way.

The big break in JJ's murder was about to come.

SEVENTEEN

Roland hadn't slept. The cocaine and the thoughts of near death kept him perpetually energized. In fact, the cocaine was still in the room. Ashley had forgotten it in her rush to leave. Roland took it and placed it in the digital safe. It may be useful to pass the time before the god-awful traitor got there.

The sun had come up three hours ago. He was starting to feel the drain of the night on him and thought he should sleep. Moving over to the bed, he got undressed and plopped onto the California King-sized mattress. Roland was fast asleep in mere moments.

...

My sister had left to go to work. She had little vacation time and had to use it sparingly as a single mother. Before leaving her home, she informed me that she would be working a half day and would be back in the early afternoon. My sister told me numerous times not to give her niece any more sweets and to make sure she took her nap at around noon.

After I watched hours of cartoons with my niece and had tickle fights, my phone rang.

"Hello," I answered.

"Hey, it's me," Boweiler, my neighbor who constantly used my bathroom, proclaimed.

"Is something wrong?" I asked since I did not expect a call from him.

"I don't know," he responded.

He went on to tell me about the large, tattooed man who claimed to be my brother. I informed him that my brother was tall but not large in the way Boweiler had described. My brother didn't have any tattoos either.

"Well, I just thought I would let you know," he asserted.

"Thanks," I said as we hung up.

...

Casey Eisenstein, the engineering student who had made Roland's crutch, arrived at the station. He got to the steps of the building and paused. What if they charge me with a crime? He thought. Kevin Roland was a billionaire, are they even going to believe me? he wondered. Casey stood on the steps and contemplated his next move. The student knew what the ethical thing to do was, but he lingered wondering if there were some easier path he could take.

It is always the right time do the right thing, he said to himself as he charged up the steep steps. He told the officer at the entry desk that he had information about the Juan Jackson murder and needed to talk to someone right away. The police officer told him to have a seat and someone would be down shortly to speak with him.

...

It was time for my niece's nap. I tried to put her in bed and leave to get some things done. She would have none of it. I was to stay with her until she fell asleep, she informed me. Lying down in the bed, I feared I would fall asleep. I hadn't slept much last night, and a nap wouldn't hurt. But, I had a pressing issue. I needed to the call the police and inform them of the intruder that had been in my condo.

···

But to continue:

The female officer in charge of the murder case came and met the young, engineering student. She could tell that he was nervous.

"Let's go to my office," she told him.

They walked upstairs without speaking. Casey had so much he wanted to say, but he wasn't sure when he was supposed to say it. He remained quiet.

The female detective was giving the potential witness his space. She didn't want to crowd him. Until he brought it up, she would let him think and reflect on what he had to say. They arrived at her office, and she gestured for him to have one of the two seats in front of her messy desk. He sat.

Still standing, she broke the silence, "I'm gonna run and get some coffee, can I get you anything? Coffee? Water? Soda?" The detective wanted to make him as comfortable as possible.

"Some cold water would be nice," Casey responded nervously.

"Okay, I'll be right back, and we can chat," the officer said as she left the office.

The female detective came back with the drinks.

Casey opened up and told her his story. How he constructed the crutch, that the buyer had asked that the spring be strong enough to penetrate a steel toed boot, that the trigger for the mechanism be hidden in the handle, how much he was paid, how long it took to make, and who had requested it and paid for it, all came from his mouth fluidly. He didn't leave out a single detail.

"Kevin Dewayne Roland, the billionaire," the detective said with a smile.

Casey misinterpreted the woman's smile for contempt or mockery.

"No, really, it was him," the engineer asserted.

The female detective realized that he thought she didn't believe him.

"Casey, I believe you, I do," she said sincerely.

...

Listen:

My niece was asleep. I had dozed off but only for a moment. Sliding my arm out from under the sleeping child, I got out of bed. I walked down the hallway and headed to the living room. My phone was lying on the counter. I grabbed and started to dial the detective in charge of JJ's case.

It hit me. Another thought bubble. I shook violently. Fight it, I told myself, you need to locate a pen and paper. As if doing some new age dance, I trembled as I wobbled in search of writing materials. Finding them, I wrote. The first line read:
Casey Eisenstein was a young engineering student at the only university in Ilium.
The event came to a rapid halt after I got six lines onto the page. I booted my laptop and added them to the file of all the previous words that had rushed from me. Perusing them again, I sought a pattern. But, none came.

Relieved that the outbreak had passed, I called the detective to report the tattooed man in my condo.

...

"Am I in trouble?" Casey asked childishly.

"You didn't commit any crime that I'm aware of," the female detective noted, "you just made something for someone." She was right. Casey had not made a bomb or any other illegal item, so he would not be charged with any crime.

"Let's…" the female detective began, but she was cut off by her phone ringing. She held up one finger to Casey to tell him they would get back to things in a moment. The amber of the moment was thickening.

"Hello?" she answered the phone.

"Okay, yeah, really, uh huh," she said to the voice on the other end.

"Well, I think we should do two things," she stated assertively.

"First, we will have a sketch artist stop by and have your neighbor help in constructing a sketch. Second, with your permission, we will dust your place for prints," the detective announced.

"Yeah, just send me an email that states that we have permission to enter your condo," she said as she gave out her email address to the person on the other end of the line. That person was me, and I would send an email two minutes after disconnecting the call.

...

Roland was in the middle of a sexual dream about Ashley and her twin. Well, not her actual twin, who was a guy, but a female who was a carbon copy of Ashley. A carbon copy is an old expression used when a paper was duplicated using a carbon layering system. Now, there were digital copies, and the carbon process had been relegated to duplication history. As an expression, carbon copy worked for noting the similarity in twins though. Both were carbon life forms.

In the dream, he had four arms. Two were choking the life out of Ashley's twin. The other two were unhooking Ashley's bra. He couldn't tell which was causing him a greater rush. Roland was jolted out of the dream by the perpetual ringing of his cellphone.

"What!?" he said perturbed, wishing he had more time within the dreamscape.

The shady, private investigator informed him that the person that Roland sought had checked out of a hotel in Philadelphia the other day.

"There's more," the voice said, "but it'll cost ya."

Roland was in no mood to be swindled more. He told the guy that he would pay him the usual rate and to "take it or leave it."

"Okay, okay," the investigator came back defensively. The private investigator had a mole who was a technician in the Digital Evidence Analysis Department of Ilium's PD. The police didn't mind using the acronym PD for Police Department, but the technicians refused to be called DEAD. It seems some acronyms are more likeable than others.

The investigator told Roland that a technician had recently been working to analyze audio clips that had Roland's voice. He didn't know why, but the mole had told the investigator he would contact him as soon as he knew more.

...

The female detective hung up the phone and returned to address Casey. He was fidgeting with the water bottle's cap.

"Okay, where were we?" she began, "Oh yeah, let's…" A hard knock on her door interrupted the sentence.

The technician working to analyze the voice patterns of Tyler Greene and Kevin Roland entered. He began explaining the process of his analysis. Removing static, cleaning the digital files, extracting external noises, delimiting other voices, file absorption rates, margin of error analysis, deletion of potential confounding variables, he was saying as if giving a lecture on the intricacies of his job. The technician was socially awkward and didn't realize what information was attractive and necessary to the female detective and what was useless. It was part of the reason he was cast off into technical arena of police work.

"Get to the point," the female detective demanded after patiently waiting for the outcome.

"It appears that there is a 99.82% match in the two vocal clips," he stated, and added, "I also used facial recognition software to establish that the two individuals are strikingly similar, at a rate of 96%."

The female detective was excited. She stood up.

Pointing at the technician, she asserted, "You, go print up the results and bring them back to me immediately. I need to use them to get a warrant."

"You," she noted in a softer tone, pointing to Casey, "come with me."

She took Casey to the male detective on the case and had Casey regurgitate his story. Afterwards, she told her male colleague the details of the technical analysis.

"So, you think a billionaire killed a public defender in broad daylight," the male detective said mockingly. He was always critical of her, but, in this case, he could not conceive of a potential motivation for the act.

"What motive do we have?" he asserted bluntly.

The female detective told him that they didn't need to determine the motive right now, they needed to get more evidence and a search warrant should provide that. A search warrant allowed law enforcement to search a person's home. They were needed because of the Fourth Amendment of the Constitution. Lately, the government didn't seem to need warrants. They had the Patriot Act. It worked like a search warrant.

"Isn't this all a little circumstantial," the officer said to her, "maybe we shouldn't get our panties all in a bind."

Casey snickered.

The female detective made clear that she was going to *the* judge for a warrant with or without her colleague's help. The judge was the Honorable Harold Lawson. As a judge, Lawson would give a warrant to any law enforcement who requested one. The Ilium PD used him sparingly because they were worried he may be removed from the bench for such indiscretion.

...

The thing was:

The female detective working the Juan Jackson murder didn't realize that Roland was tracking me now, so she never called to inform me that Tyler Greene and

236

Kevin Roland appeared to be the same person. Even if she had, it would not have helped much. Roland was masquerading now as Paul Venters, the businessman, or Luke Taylor, the tattooed body builder.

...

But to continue:

Roland was disturbed by the recent call he had received. He went to the digital safe and retrieved that cocaine. Pouring out a small pile, he did two lines. The rush removed his doubts and insecurities. He was invincible again. Roland headed down the private elevator to have some food. He got some steak and lobster at the hotel restaurant and drank some wine. Life was good.

After gambling for a few hours, he realized he was bored. He was about even and lacked the rush from the previous night's affairs. Roland went back to his room to plan an adventure for the night. Evening was upon Sin City, and he planned to enjoy it.

He would kill himself a prostitute. Hookers were like homeless individuals, society seemed to look the other way when one came up missing. A prostitute would be easy to find in this desert oasis. Even though it was legal to be a prostitute in Nevada, the city of Las Vegas was an exception. With all the tourists, it did not stop many down-on-their-luck individuals from taking on the oldest profession.

Roland dressed as Paul Venter again. He didn't want to scare a woman into not trusting him, and Luke Taylor's size may do just that. Opening up his duffle bag, he grabbed a knife, a blindfold, and some rope. He called a rental car company and requested an SUV. The letters SUV stood for Sport Utility Vehicle. It was another acronym. Cars didn't use too many acronyms even though they often had letters to designate them. RX-7, 300Z, STX, RSX, CTS, WRX, and numerous others were letters that appeared to randomly be selected to describe a model.

A representative of the rental car company came to the hotel and picked him up. They drove to the company's address. The attendant at the counter asked for his license. Roland gave him *his* license. In his coked-out state, he had forgotten to pick up Venter's wallet.

"Didn't you say a reservation for a Paul Venter?" the attendant questioned.

"Yeah, Paul's my business partner," Roland said dressed as Venter with a voice modulating to Venter's tone, "I'm Kevin Roland."

"The billionaire?" the attendant came back quizzically.

"Oh, no, I wish," Roland proclaimed. It was a lie. Like you, I hate being lied to.

"You probably get that all the time, huh?" the attendant responded.

"Not as much as you might think."

"Well, you don't look much like him."

"Yeah, we just share the same name."

"So, will Mr. Venter be driving the vehicle too?"

"No, just me," Roland said with a smile.

...

It was getting late, and my sister's babysitter had not arrived yet. My sister and I had plans to go out for the night. I had to leave in the morning to drive to St. Louis and see our dad.

"I'm sure she'll be here any moment," my sister said with a bit of concern.

"Do we have a reservation for this place we're going to."

"No, I just don't want to miss the opening act" The doorbell rang, and the babysitter apologized profusely for being late. It seemed traffic was heavier than usual.

My sister and I got in her car and headed to the place my sister described as "a tacky talent show." A half hour later, we entered a place called Slapstick. The sign in front announced that it was best place for amateur comedy and magic.

Following my sister to a table near the stage, I saw oddities that didn't appear to create any rational pattern. On the wall was a whistle that looked as if it had come from a train or steamboat. It looked like this:

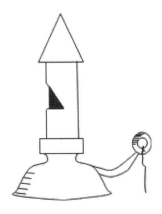

Next to the whistle was one of the many metal torches with a red light bulb shaped like a flame that lined the walls. It looked like this:

We sat down and ordered some beers. My sister was giddy. Being a single parent, she didn't get to go out very often. When she had a chance, she always tried to come to this place. I was anxious to see the show since she talked it up so much.

The show combined magicians and comedians. The first act was atrocious. A chubby, white guy wearing a jacket that said "Innocent bystander" was making fun of Black people. His jacket looked like this:

The overweight man was joking that no Blacks were innocent and deserved what they got for living in the crime-filled ghetto. I wanted to leave, but I knew my sister didn't get to have adult time often. Uncomfortable, I hoped the next act would be better.

Using a handkerchief, the next act did a bit of magic. It was a nice contrast to the idiot who started the show. During one trick, the magician made his finger disappear. It looked like this:

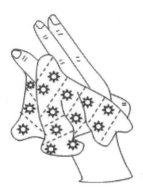

His finger reappeared. It was all just a trick, a lie. Like you, I hate being lied to. But, I enjoyed this act of deception.

The best part of the show was not any of the acts. It was watching my sister laugh and enjoy herself. She had been suffering from anxiety for a while, and it was nice to see her relax and relish life.

...

Roland went back to the hotel and quickly switched out his wallets. He now had the right wallet for Paul Venter. Driving the shady side of Sin City, he began his quest to find and kill a hooker.

Roland never accomplished his task for the night. After passing a group of scantly clad women on the corner of a block, he backtracked to pick one up. On his next pass, a police officer pulled him over.

The officer ran the plates of the car and found that it was rental reserved to Kevin Roland. Going to the driver's window, he requested license and registration. Paul Venter gave him his ID and told him it was a rental.

"Can you give me directions?" Venter asked the officer, "I'm lost."

The officer looked at him suspiciously. Tourists always seemed to get "lost" in the shady part of town.

"I'll give you some in a second," he stated, "let me run this really quick to see that it clears." The officer needed to know if the person had any bench warrants on their record. Paul Venters persona was fairly clean compared to the other identities that Roland used. The only thing on Venters' record was a ticket for having a tail light out. That event was fiction. It never had happened. Roland had constructed it to make the persona a little more believable. It was a lie. Like you, I hate being lied to.

The police officer came back and gave the poor tourist directions back to the strip. Roland realized that if he got caught now, he would not be able to kill the traitor. He needed to be smarter with his choices, he thought.

…

The two detectives working the Juan Jackson case, along with four police officers, stood at the gates of Roland's mansion. The female detective rang the buzzer.

"Can I help you?" the voice of Roland's maid came over the intercom.

The detective informed her that they had a warrant to search the premises, and the maid should open the gate. The maid had no problems with law enforcement and respected them dearly. In fact, her cousin was an officer in the Ilium PD. Coincidentally, he was the mole that the shady, private investigator used to get information from within the department.

The police entered and showed the maid the warrant. The group spent hours combing the vast space for any evidence that would link the billionaire, Kevin Roland, to the murder of Juan Jackson. They were about to leave when the female detective saw the entrance to Roland's mancave.

"That's a lot of security," she said to her colleague, "I want to know what's on the other side." They called in a technician from the Ilium department. When he got there, the technician looked over the security for about twenty minutes.

"You need a *real* specialist," the technician asserted, "call the FBI."

The female detective got on the phone and called the FBI to request that a security specialist be sent to their location. The FBI informed her that they were underfunded and overworked. It would be almost a week before a specialist could be sent. After arriving on sight, the specialist would still need two days to crack the various layers of security. In nine days, they would be inside Roland's mancave. I didn't have nine days. Roland would break into my hotel room to kill me in less than that.

The Ilium department decided it would be best to station an officer at the residence to secure the sight until they could see what was behind that mysterious door.

By the time they got into his lair, Roland would be long gone, the female detective thought. She was right.

EIGHTEEN

Roland got back to his suite and decided it was best if he just go to bed. It was only a few more days until the traitor arrived, and Roland didn't want to mess up the opportunity to kill him. He slept in the large bed. No dreams came to him, but he would wake rested and rejuvenated.

...

After a night of laughs, my sister and I headed back to her place to get some rest. I would be leaving early tomorrow. In the morning, my sister made sure that my energetic niece would not wake me.

I woke refreshed. Leaving would be difficult, I had not seen my sister and niece for a couple years, and I didn't know when I would see them again. I packed my things and took them out to my luxury rental car. After tears and hugs and goodbyes, I left and headed to the St. Louis area.

...

Impatiently, the female detective waited in her office for the day to come when the specialist from the FBI would finally show up. It would take six more days, but it felt like forever.

She also was waiting for Casey Eisenstein to return. The detective had requested that he make a statement that could, if necessary, serve as a deposition. Not wanting to leave anything to luck, the detective felt she needed to attain a signed, written account of Casey's testimony. Life was unpredictable. He could end up having an accident on his scooter. The detective didn't want to leave their case to chance.

...

Roland's maid did not have his cell number. Few people did. She called the company who employed her and told them that the police had served a warrant and Mr. Roland should be told about it. The company called the number they had as a contact for him. That contact called another contact, who actually had Roland's number. Roland had set up multiple layers, like an onion, to keep his calls to a minimum and to distinguish pressing issues from insignificant ones.

He had just gotten out of a hot shower when the phone rang. Roland went to the phone and answered it.

"It's me again," the shady, private investigator stated bluntly.

"Let me guess, you want more money, and have useful information for me," Roland said half-heartedly.

"No, I'm passing information from your maid."

"What? My maid? Whatever would be so pressing that you should disturb my joyful solitude," Roland asserted annoyed.

"The police have served a search warrant and have a man stationed at your home. They are awaiting a specialist from the FBI to get into some security area you have that they can't access."

Roland was speechless.

"You still there," the investigator said.

"Yeah, yeah," Roland mumbled. He wanted to get off the line and get his defenses in place, but he also wanted to know if there was any other news for him.

"Nope, nothing else, but I will call when I find out more," the investigator stated. They hung up.

...

Listen:

I drove from the urban mammoth that was Chicago through the plains farmland of central Illinois to the St. Louis area. A small, railroad town called Prairie Du Pont was my destination. I had been raised there. It was within the St. Louis metropolitan area, but it didn't seem much like a suburb. As a municipality it was odd. Prairie Du Pont had as many churches as taverns, one restaurant, farmland randomly scattered across it, a railroad switch yard, two gas stations, and an Interstate highway running next to it. The fifteen bars and churches made sure that residents of the town of 4000 were light-hearted drinkers who did not forget their ethics and asked for forgiveness on Sunday mornings for their various escapades on Friday and Saturday nights.

Getting off of Interstate 255 at Exit 9, I drove on the main road through town past the lone high school. Every time I made it back to my hometown, I had to stop and eat at Dairy Land, the one restaurant housed in the town of drunkards and Christian. It was a tradition. Not quite a mile off the interstate, I turned left into their small parking lot and walked into the side door to what appeared more like a house than a diner. A sign on the wall reminded me that not only did they serve quick food like hamburgers, corn dogs, sloppy joes, and chicken nuggets but they also had a variety of frozen treats for desert. The sign looked like this:

IT'S HARD TO BE

UNHAPPY WHEN YOU

ARE HAVING

KRYPTONITE

ICE CREAM

The friendly woman working the counter said, "Long time, no see." She and her husband ran the place and graduated within a few years of me from the local, high school. I was somewhat dumbfounded that she still remembered me. Ahh, one of the perks of a small town.

The place had expanded in size, but it had kept almost all of its historic charms. Arcade games like Ms. Pacman and Donkey Kong still sat against the far wall propositioning young boys for their quarters. I placed my order and noticed something different behind the counter. It stood out because it looked shiny and new. The object was a fire extinguisher and had the word "Excelsior" written on it. It looked like this:

The word flooded my mind with an explosion of superfluous connections. The popular TV show, Friends, had a character named Rachel who had a poster with the word on it. In the Star Trek world, it was the specific name of a Starship in the Starfleet. It was the title to a poem by Longfellow as well as another by Whitman. The first two connections came from my watching too much television as a teenager. The last two came from Dr. Twane's lecture at Harvard on literary devices. Twane was also the one to note that railroad tracks symbolized destiny. I was now in a town full of tracks.

The co-owner brought my food out to me, and I devoured it. I was not simply hungry but pressed for time. My dad would be home soon, and I wanted to see him the moment he arrived back from work. He was retired but still worked part-time. The recession had hit just about everyone in America. Well, except billionaires like Kevin Roland.

As I left Dairy Land and headed to my rental car, I noticed I would be unable to get out of the small parking lot. A truck had parked in such a manner as to block three cars from escaping. Mine was the middle one in the parking lot jail. The truck looked like this:

I went back inside and made an announcement to see if the driver was in there eating. He was. The red-bearded, freckle-faced, young driver apologized for his act.

"There weren't no place to park," he said.

"I know, the lot is small," I replied trying to show him I fully understood.

...

The thing was:

Roland became restless. He needed to find a way to keep the authorities out of his mancave. There was enough evidence throughout the lair to put him away for life. Fraud, forgery, conspiracy, assault, and murder were only the first charges that came to Roland's mind, but that was far from a complete list. If the FBI entered the mancave, they would have evidence enough to charge him with 87 different, felony charges. He had to stop them.

Focusing his attention on the problem at hand, Roland grabbed his phone and called his salvation. Roland's attorney informed him that he would immediately get a cease and desist established against the warrant. The attorney made clear that he had the necessary connections to, at least, keep the FBI out of Roland's private residence until a hearing could take place. Moreover, the lawyer asserted that tomorrow morning he would request discovery to access the evidence against Roland that allowed for the warrant in the first place.

Roland sighed in relief as he hung up the phone. The fire had temporarily been stalled. With good legal maneuvering, it may disappear entirely, Roland hoped.

He decided that he would not gamble tonight but would go to a show. There were always numerous entertainers working the Vegas scene. Roland remembered that the front desk had brochures listing all the nightly attractions. Putting on his shoes, he grabbed his wallet and headed to the elevator. His phone rang.

"Hello?" Roland answered.

"Hello," a female voice said slyly on the other end.

"Who is this?" Roland demanded. Before the voice responded, Roland had determined the caller. It was the cosmetic artist who had sold him all the wigs, moustaches, color contacts, height manipulators, voice modulators, tattoo kits, jewelry, clothes, fake scars, hollow casts, finger nails, plastic noses and ears, and an assortment of other costume effects.

"Nevermind," he said, "how did you get this number, Stella?"

Stella laughed. "I have my ways," she reported. It had taken her quite a lot of time and money to simply get Roland's number, and she planned to recoup it all and more. In fact, she had located the shady, private investigator, who himself was not easy to find. Given his recent hospitalization caused by not paying his gambling debts, he was extremely open to her bribe. Other people had the number too, so the investigator thought he would be above suspicion.

"Why are you calling me?" Roland said frustrated that someone had managed to call him on the line he limited to few people.

"Five million," she said flatly.

"Huh."

"You wire five million dollars to the account I established in the Cayman's"

"Why?"

"Because I saw the video of the guy with the crutch that killed that public defender, and I know it was you."

Roland laughed. "Why would I do that?" He tried to sound mocking but the nervousness in his voice came through.

"I could care less," she asserted, "you have until tomorrow at 5 pm, I will check the account then. If it is not in there, I'm going straight to the police with *all* my information." She hung up.

The embers of Rome's blaze were starting to catch fire. Too bad Roland didn't have the Excelsior fire extinguisher with him. He could have put out a fire quickly. Roland did, however, have a contact that would solve his issue.

...

I drove to my childhood home at 316 Rock Road. All the roads in town were named either after the railroad or the two limestone quarries. Lime Street, Granite Drive, Conductor Boulevard, Stone Street, Quarry Road, and Caboose Center were all streets in the neighborhood where I grew up.

"I'm gettin' too old to go hunting," my dad said.

"How about fishing?" I asked.

We were trying to plan the few hours I had with him tomorrow. I would have to leave by late afternoon or early evening, and we wanted to do something together.

"By the way," he added, "do you still have grandpa's shotgun?"

I told him I had it and kept it well maintained. It was in the trunk of the rental car outside.

"I can't recall, was that a 12, 28, or 20 gauge?" he said. His memory had gotten poorer with old age.

"12, dad, 12," I replied. I was unsure why I repeated the number. My dad had excellent hearing.

"Oh, in that case, I got some shells for it that've been lying around here for years." He retrieved the shells and handed them to me. There were six of them. They were double aught buck. Double aught buckshot was used to hunt larger game like deer and could deter or kill a bear if it charged. A male deer was called a buck, so they called the round "buckshot." I put the six rounds in my front pocket.

I finally convinced my dad to go fishing with me the next day. He and I went to the pole barn and got all the fishing gear out and ready. I felt like I was twelve again.

...

Roland went to the front desk and got tickets to a famous magician that was performing at the hotel across the street. The performance would be much more spectacular than the one that my sister and I saw at Slapstick. He got in the private elevator to go back to his penthouse. Roland needed privacy. He was about to call and put a hit on Stella.

Roland called the one person he knew would take care of any task for the right price. Tank Rizo had once raped a Midwestern senator for Roland. The billionaire went to his duffle bag and retrieved the voice modulator. He adjusted it to the vocal settings of Katie Holiday, the persona that Rizo had worked for back then. In the voice of Holiday, Roland contacted Rizo, explained the task at hand, the payment, and the deadline. Rizo accepted less money than his previous job because there was little travel and, unlike rape, murder didn't leave a witness. Before the 5pm deadline, Roland's henchman had hunted and killed Stella. So it goes.

Another fire extinguished, Rome would stand another day.

...

My dad and I got up before sunrise and drove to a small lake that we had fished at many times. On the forty minute drive, we talked and caught up. We kept in touch over the phone, but there was something more genuine to conversation when it was face-to-face.

Fishing for most of the morning and early afternoon, we had a good haul. Well, my dad did, at least. He caught four bass, two catfish, a crappie, and three bluegill. I caught a gar and a bluegill.

We returned to my childhood home. I said my goodbyes and told him that I loved him, he gave me a hug.

I headed to the Kansas City area to meet up with my childhood friend. We were to go hunting tomorrow, but I still had to drive the four hours over to his place. I called him to tell him that I was leaving St. Louis and would be there in about four hours. He told me that he would save some of his wife's good cooking for me. To make sure I was a good visitor, I would have to refrain from stopping to grab dinner, and the ham sandwich I had while fishing would have to tie me over. I hopped on Interstate 70 and headed west.

...

My childhood friend, Floyd, was waiting for me when I pulled into his driveway. He owned a modest house, had an easygoing wife, two dogs, and no kids. I got out of the luxury car and was mugged by two, happy Golden Retrievers.

"Get down," Floyd shouted, and the dogs instantly obeyed.

As he walked from his front porch over to see if I needed any help with my bags, I realized that I had not seen him for almost ten years. We took my stuff inside, sat, ate leftovers from he and his wife's dinner, and drank a beer. Our conversation was easy as if we had only seen each other yesterday.

"So, I brought my grandpa's gun, what are we gonna hunt?" I asked.

"Sorry, should of told ya on the phone, but nothing I hunt is in season yet."

"That's okay"

"Well, I thought, we'd just go skeet shooting tomorrow, if ya like."

I told him that sounded like a great plan.

NINETEEN

The next morning, Floyd's wife cooked a big breakfast. Biscuits and gravy, eggs, sausage, bacon, pancakes, waffles, toast, and five kinds of jam ordained the table. I couldn't recall the last time I had a home-cooked breakfast as magnificent. It was delicious, too. I complimented her endlessly on her creation. She sincerely denied that it was anything special. And so on.

Floyd and I got our fill and headed out to the local skeet shooting range. The name given to skeet shooting was odd. Skeet, as a word, was an old form of the word "shoot" or "to shoot." So, in essence, we were going to go shoot shooting. It seemed a little redundant to me, maybe even overkill. To remove this repetition, some people had called it trap shooting. It was yet another odd expression. Trap was a slang word for mouth. For example, "Shut your trap." So, we were going to go mouth shooting.

"So, do you go clay pigeon shooting often?" I asked on the ride to the range.

"It's called skeet shootin'," he responded, "and I go about once a month, maybe twice a month."

"So, you're pretty good at clay pigeon shooting" I half-stated, half-asked.

"Stop it, call it skeet or trap shooting, you're being silly and sound like a city boy."

"Oh, we're not going clay pigeon shooting," I questioned with a smile. I just couldn't get myself to go shoot shooting or mouth shooting. Before this was all over, someone would likely get shot in the mouth, and I hoped it wasn't me.

I had brought my grandpa's shotgun to go hunting with Floyd. He informed me, however, that the barrel length of my side-by-side, double-barrel would make it less effective for skeet shooting. He let me borrow his over-and-under, 12-gauge. At the range, we did all 8 positions multiple times. Floyd was quite efficient. He averaged 24 of 25. I was not so great and averaged 7 of 25. Almost all the ones I actually hit were ones closest in proximity to me. Distance was not my cup of tea, as they say.

We headed back to his house for lunch. Waiting for Floyd's wife to finish the last pieces of the meal, Floyd and I talked about days gone by. Adventures from our childhood sprang to mind effortlessly, and we laughed at our past escapades. As I started to tell another tale of our youth, it hit me. Another thought bubble. I shook violently.

"You okay," Floyd asked as he rushed to my side. I fought back and struggled against the sensations bombarding my mind and body.

"I'll...be...fine," I struggled to get out as I got up and located a piece of paper and pen. I wrote fast. The first sentence read:
As I left Dairy Land and headed to my rental car, I noticed I would be unable to get out of the small parking lot.

Eight more sentences and a crude image drawn by hand completed the moment. The outburst had passed. I looked down and read the words. They were a memory from just the other day. Floyd could tell I seemed confused. He read over my shoulder text written on the page and examined the simple drawing of a truck.

"What was that all about?"

"It's nothing. I'll be okay."

"Did you go to Dairy Land when you were back in Prairie Du Pont?"

"Yeah, yeah, I did," I mumbled still trying to grasp the issue that kept consuming me.

"So, why'd you write that?"

"I don't know, Floyd, I just don't know."

"Do you always shake like you're havin' a convulsion like your possessed before you write about your past?"

I explained to him that the writing was not always my past. Sometimes, it was just pieces of some story or someone else's life. It didn't make sense, and, as far as I knew, there was no cure for it. Being one of my best friends, I opened up and told him about pissing myself and puking on some people in a restaurant. I could tell he wanted to laugh, but he controlled himself.

"You got quite a problem there," he asserted. Floyd tried to convince me not to drive anymore because he feared what would occur if I were on the road when it happened again. I assured him I would be fine. He told me that it may be wise to leave my shotgun at his place since firearms and medical conditions don't mix well. I was not going to part with my grandpa's gun. I trusted Floyd with my life, but the old double-barrel was the only thing I had from my grandpa. Floyd told me to call if I needed anything, and he would come get me no matter where I was. I thanked him.

I would have to get on the road soon. Driving to Denver from Kansas City would take me eight hours or more. I was luck the rental car company allotted me unlimited miles. After another delicious home-cooked meal, I said my goodbyes and took off down Interstate 70 west.

...

Roland didn't know what to do and was bored. He had money and time but no imagination. Earlier in the day, he had received two calls that made him elated. The first call was from a contact that had been informed by Rizo that "the problem was taken care of." Stella was dead. So it goes.

The second call was from his trusted attorney. The lawyer made clear that the cease and desist would keep the law out of his home until the upcoming hearing. The judge had set the hearing for a week from tomorrow. It was plenty of time to kill the traitor, hope on a flight, and proclaim his innocence, Roland thought.

...

But to continue:

On my drive to Denver, I was lucky not to get a ticket. The flat plains of Kansas and Eastern Colorado begged for speed. There was little around but vast farmland, and I consistently went 15 to 20 mph over the posted limit. The few other cars on the highway appeared to be doing the same thing. I took it as a sign that it was okay, even if it was illegal.

I got to my hotel in Denver a little before 9pm. Kicking off my shoes, I sat on the bed for a moment to relax. It felt good to just let my feet breathe. Feet didn't really breathe, but it was an expression.

Originally, I had scheduled to get to bed early when I arrived in Denver because the next day I would be driving the 11-hour nightmare section of my journey to Las Vegas. I decided, however, to change my plans. I'll just go out tonight, enjoy myself, and sleep in, I thought. Since I was going to make it to Vegas late, I didn't know why I should splurge there on a high end hotel. I'll just cancel the reservation, I thought. I picked up my cellphone to call the hotel on the Vegas strip and found that the battery was dead. So it goes.

In fact, my cellphone was malfunctioning and not holding a charge. My charger was to blame. It was faulty. The car charger I brought with me was a little better, but the phone was likely on its last leg. Phones didn't have legs. It was just an expression.

I opened my laptop and reserved a room at a cheap inn off the strip. Getting in late, I would only really need a bed to sleep on. I decided I would splurge tonight and when I got to Los Angeles and saw my brother.

After showering and shaving, I got dressed and headed for a night on the town. I stopped at the front desk to ask the attendant for a place to go drink and have fun. The attendant asked if I was looking for strip club, bar, night club, or pub. I told him that it didn't really matter as long as it was unique.

"Oh, if you want unique, then you have to go to Et Cetera," he claimed.

"Okay, where is it?"

"Take a left out our front door, walk three blocks, take another left, and it will be half way down the block on your right."

"Thanks," I said as I walked away. I stopped and walked back.

"Do they have a dress code? I mean, is this okay to wear," I questioned as I gestured to my attire.

"They let anything any," he smiled, "and I mean anything."

I stopped in the lobby of my hotel at the ATM and withdrew some cash. Then, I followed the directions provided. I knew I was at the place when I saw a line of disparate individuals and a sign that read:

I got in line behind a tall, slender guy with a spiked Mohawk. He had on a baby blue, tank top, ripped jean shorts, and combat boots. The girl next to him wasn't even wearing a shirt. Literally, she had nothing on but black leather pants and bright pink stiletto heels.

I felt someone tap me on the shoulder. I turned.

"Uh, you look new to the scene," the chubby guy, wearing a Hawaiian shirt and endless Mardi Gras beads, asserted.

"Just visiting the area, and was told this place is unique."

"Yeah, they like self-expression in here," he said smiling.

"Is there a cover?" I asked ignorantly.

"Yes and no."

"What?"

"You see, it's like this. If you're new or give the wrong answer at the door to Bluebeard, you get charged twenty-five bucks to get in."

"Really?" I said astounded.

"But," he continued, "if your answer is right, the cover is free."

"So, what's the right answer? And who's Bluebeard?"

"Depends on the people in front of you," the chubby guy said as he waved over two of his girlfriends to cut in line where he was.

"Look," he continued, "it's a word game. The person in front of you will give a word to Bluebeard as their answer to 'what's the password?' If they say 'cat', then you gotta pick any word that start with T"

"Why T?" I questioned as the line steadily moved forward.

"Cause their answer ends with T, silly," he said laughing. "Tourists," he mumbled to his two girlfriends.

"Listen, then old Bluebeard is gonna ask me what the password is. If you answered 'toad', then I gotta come up with a D word."

I understood the game to get free cover and was glad this guy had helped me.

"Two last questions," I said, as the line moved me closer to the entrance.

"I feel like I owe you, can I buy you a drink when we get inside?"

"Sure, I'll be over in the VIP section, what's your second question?"

"Who's Bluebeard?"

"Ah, you'll know'em when you see'em."

The VIP with two girlfriends was right. As I entered the club, I saw a seven foot giant wearing a jacket with a front pocket that seemed a size too small. The jacket looked like this:

The giant's hair was dyed green and beard dyed blue. It reminded me of an old superstition:

> Beware of that man
> Be he friend or brother,
> Whose hair is one color
> And moustache another.

"What's the password?" Bluebeard growled in a loud, intimidating voice.

The guy in front of me had answered with "closet," so I answered the question with "trigger."

"No cover," Bluebeard's voice stated to the half-naked women working the register behind him.

Over the next few hours, I drank and danced and had fun. The place was eclectic. People wore togas, zoot suits, body paint, leather, gothic attire, and array of clothes that made it feel not only unique but open to the range of human expression. The crowd was electric and their energy high. Bar patrons were friendly. Some were stoned. They were not quite as energetic. Marijuana was legal in Colorado. Maybe getting high from time to time had made Coloradans more relaxed and free-spirited. Before I left, I remembered to pay the VIP section a visit and buy the Hawaiian-shirt-wearing gentleman a beer. He thanked me, and I was on my way.

A little tipsy, I staggered back to my hotel and went to sleep.

TWENTY

It wasn't until early afternoon that I awoke. I was getting too old for late night escapades. Hurriedly, I showered and packed. The hotel was not very forgiving of my late check out. I had to pay them some more money. Reflecting on the night at Et Cetera, I felt it was worth it. I packed the rental car and jumped on, what had become a common route for me, interstate 70. Heading to Vegas, I would have to catch interstate 15 in the state of Industry.

Pulling over on the side of the highway, I searched my cellphone for the number to the upscale hotel on the Vegas strip where I had a reservation. My phone was not working. The battery was still dead. So it goes.

I plugged it into the car charger, told myself I would call when I stopped for dinner, and merged back onto the freeway.

...

At the same time, seven years ago:

The Thought Transfer Project had completed its mission to collect thoughts from participants. Not all of the fifteen hundred participants would make it to the project facility. One of the ones who *did* make it would not live long enough to have her thoughts stored. So it goes. Some would be incompatible with the process, and their thoughts were lost to history. A few had their ideas stored. Many of the successful participants would have adverse effects occur to them. Neurological disorders, psychological disruptions, and physical disabilities would abound in the group. One of them was famous. He had volunteered for such torture. His name was Kurt Vonnegut.

As Lead Researcher and Facilities Director, Dr. Darnell Durling Heath had made the project of thought transfer run as effectively as possible given the various circumstances that arose. He made the body of a French woman who had committed suicide disappear, had institutionalized hundreds of participants with mental effects caused by the machine, and had sent hundred more to therapy for nerve damage to their appendages. The only celebrity participant had also acquired a negative effect. The fluid in his ear was continually thickening. Ear fluid ratio was significant for balance.

Heath headed to go talk to the celebrity.

•••

Roland decided to take in another show on the night that the traitor was to make it into town. He figured he should enjoy his time in Sin City, and he could kill the traitor after the show. Roland went to the front desk and perused the listings. A famous singer was performing, and Roland purchased VIP seating and a backstage pass. He paid the bell boy to retrieve his tickets and pass. Roland headed back to his room to plan out the night and the murder. He told the bell boy to leave the tickets at the front desk, and he would retrieve them before the show.

The gopher was happy at the added job. The young man need only go to the ticket counter on the other end of the massive hotel. It would take him fifteen minutes. For his labor, the bell boy would have a hundred bucks. He liked how people splurged in Vegas.

•••

I was in St. George, Utah when I decided to stop and have dinner. It was quite late, but I had seen few towns and cities with any semblance of a place to eat. St. George was the patron saint of England and was connected to farming and agriculture. George, as a name, even meant land worker or farmer. His memorial would be celebrated in just over a month. He was revered not only by the Catholic Church but also in Islam. A popular tale had him slaying a dragon. He was one cool dude.

The problem was:

Mormons didn't find that cool dude good enough. They made up their own St. George, and the city was named after him. Coincidentally, he was a farmer, too. He helped settle the Mormon town to grow cotton. The area was still called Dixie even though they no longer raised cotton. The Paiutes of southern Utah had called the Mormon, St. George Non-choko-wicher, but Bokonists would have called him a stuppa.

I had food at a truck stop diner just off the interstate. Tired from driving, I forgot to call and cancel my reservation at the upscale hotel on the strip of Sin City. It was only about another two hours, and I would be on the Strip.

TWENTY ONE

The neon lights of Vegas filled the desert sky like a simulated sunrise. Ah God, what an ugly city every city is, I thought, the unnaturalness of it all. Vegas was exceptionally ugly. It played a siren song of hope only to give despair. Everyone came to it with the thought of a bright future, only to leave it with a despicable past.

Seeing the glowing lights, I remembered that I still needed to cancel my reservation. I wasn't sure what the hotel would do or say since it was short notice, but I drove to the Strip to find out.

...

Roland left the hotel and headed to see the female vocalist for whom he had purchased tickets and a backstage pass. As he reached the edge of the sidewalk next to the street, the doorman said something. Roland turned around.

"Can I call you a cab, sir?" the doorman repeated.

"Nah, I'm not going far," Roland replied. Realizing that he had forgotten to pick up the tickets for the show, Roland headed back inside to get them from the front desk.

...

I pulled up to the curb of the upscale hotel. The valet walked over to me, expecting for me to hand him the keys to the luxury car.

"I just have to run to the front desk," I told him, "I'll be right back."

"Well, you're really not supposed to park here, even for a little while."

"I promise I'll be in and out in no time."

"Do you know how many times people tell us that?"

I was tired from the long drive and didn't want to have a lengthy conversation about parking, people's false promises, and valet service. Handing the valet fifty dollars, I told him that I would be out in ten minutes or less. If I did not make the time frame, he could keep the fifty. If I did make it, he had to give it back. He agreed to the terms. It was a sign of trust between two strangers. He trusted that I would return, and I trusted that, if I did, he would give me back my friend Grant.

...

Roland was told by the front desk worker that the bell boy had noticed that the tickets had not yet been picked up and had taken them up to Roland's penthouse. It was an act of kindness, but Roland was frustrated by it. He hopped on the private elevator to retrieve the tickets.

...

I got to the front counter and told them that I needed to cancel my reservation. The desk staff worker told me that a surcharge would be applied to the credit card that held the room. After being told the fee, I wanted to ask for a manager and get it reduced or a waiver, but I didn't. As it was, I was exhausted for the long drive. I didn't want to deal with it anymore.

Overall, I would still be saving money and had my hotel off the Strip to get some shut-eye.

As I exited the hotel, I saw the valet looking at his watch.

"You still had three minutes," he said as he smiled and returned the fifty-dollars. There was good in the world. Trust could be reciprocated by strangers.

"Thanks," I said returning his smile genuinely.

...

Roland exited the upscale hotel in time to see a luxury car with Massachusetts plates leave. He realized he liked the shade of silver the luxury car had and noted that he would have to have one of his corvettes painted in that tone.

Roland went to the concert. He was constantly distracted. His mind raced in anticipation of killing that vile traitor he had waited so long for. It was going to end, tonight. Little did he know.

...

In less than ten minutes, I had gotten from the upscale newest hotel of the Strip to my cheap hotel in the "old" part of Vegas. I checked in, got my room, and readied for bed. The eleven-hour drive from Denver had drained me. Before sleeping, I called and canceled my cheap hotel in Los Angeles and splurged by reserving a room at a five-star hotel there instead. It seemed more rational to splurge in that city since I would be there for a few days rather than in Vegas where I would only spend the night.

Peacefully, I dreamed of dancing with Blossom again. This time the dream reached greater depths

because there was no Y-O-U alarm clock to slap me out
it.

...

The thing was:
Predator and prey had nearly crossed paths, but
there was no incident. No death. So it doesn't go.
Tomorrow, the employee of Imagination
Financial Services would not be so fortunate. In less
than 24-hours, the predator and the prey would end up
in the same room, and the predator would be armed
with his deadly revolver.

...

Zac and Liz Harper-Ferry were honeymooning
in Vegas. Zac was 25, and Liz was 23. They had been
high school sweethearts. Liz wanted a tacky wedding at
the well-known, little chapel in Vegas. Zac wanted Liz
to be happy. They flew into Vegas two nights ago, got
married, and had been spending most of their time in a
hotel room that some rich guy paid for when he found
out they were newlyweds.
"Enjoy," the rich divorcee said as he called and
made the arrangement, "hell, I've enjoyed a
honeymoon eight times now." He had been married and
divorced to six, different women.
Zac and Liz took the rich man's generosity as a
sign that their union would bring good fortune. Little
did they know.

...

The female detective in charge of the Juan
Jackson investigation couldn't sleep. She had been

lying in bed for more than two hours tossing and turning. Her body could not find a comfortable position, and her mind would not stop thinking. How do I catch Kevin Roland? Where is the piece of evidence I need? What would it look like? Can I get in that room that sealed in any other way? What if Roland bolts out of the country?

That last question disturbed her almost as much as when Roland's lawyer had got a cease and desist on searching Roland's estate. The billionaire may evade any scrutiny at all. She knew he was linked to the murder. If he didn't do it, he surely knew about it in significant ways. The detective decided that she would do three things tomorrow to try to bring justice to the billionaire, who probably thought he was above the law. First, she would recruit a tech-savvy friend to try to hack into Roland's personal email. The detective wanted the information regardless of what channels were used. There may be more murders planned, and she didn't want them on her conscious. Second, she would work the legal department to freeze Roland's passport. He may be free to the roam the U.S., but she'd be damned if he got out of the country. Third, she would talk to her friend who was a judge to see if there was anyway to subpoena Mr. Kevin Roland. He may show his cards if interrogated in the right fashion. Her mind was racing so quickly to schedule her work tomorrow and conceive of other ways in which to thwart the billionaire that she didn't fall asleep for another hour.

...

But to continue:

Roland returned from the concert with a spring in his step. He rushed to his penthouse suite. He changed into the Luke Taylor persona. The large frame and tattoos would strike fear in the worthless traitor, he thought. As a costume, it took longer to ready than any of the others Roland had, but he hurried to finish the tattoos and get out the door.

Having dressed as Paul Venter earlier in the day, he had bribed a maid to get a master key to the hotel. His lockpicking gun would do no good against the electronic key entry. Grabbing the master key and hiding the gun with its silencer in the special holster for the small of his back, he headed to the private elevator and went down three floors. The traitor would be fast asleep, he thought, and would awake in terror at the form of Luke Taylor over him.

...

While standing at the doorway of the traitor's room, Luke Taylor looked quickly both ways. He inserted the master key, and the door made an inaudible click. Darting in, he closed the door quietly and stood in the dark readying himself for his triumph. He pulled out the revolver and with great stealth walked slowly to end of the hallway. The bed of the room would be just to the right around the corner. A soft light flickered in the room. Moans and groans readily came. Soft whimpering joined them.

Did the traitor have a woman with him? Roland thought. If so, both would have to die, he realized.

Luke Taylor peered into the candlelit bedroom. Two bodies were in the throes of ecstasy. The room

276

smelled of scented candles, sweat, sex, and perfume. Whoever they were, they were blissfully enjoying the amber of the moment. Roland squinted to see better in the dim light. Each body was a chiseled and youthful form. Neither was the traitor. Roland was positive he had the right room. He had come to check its place in the building on numerous occasions as he waited in Vegas for the traitor to show himself.

Roland slid the gun back into its hidden holster and watched in perverse silence the two lovers lost in their passions and bodies. He wanted to leave, but he was mesmerized by the sweaty forms glistening in the candles' flickers. His heartbeat began to quicken. He was turned on by this voyeuristic moment.

...

Zac Harper-Ferry was kissing his new wife's neck as she tilted her head back and moaned under him. He whispered how much he loved her in her ear. She responded with a deep and passionate kiss.

All of a sudden, a cellphone rang. Zac knew it was neither the ringtone of his or his new brides' phones. He paused and listened. Maybe the last hotel guest had forgotten their phone in the room. It rang again. Zac turned and saw a large man at the end of the hallway. He grabbed the nearby lamp and threw it in the direction of the stranger. Naked, he lunged from the bed toward the hall wanting to protect his love.

...

Roland was nearly drooling at the free sex show he was watching. Then, it happened. His cellphone went off. He quickly reached in his pocket to retrieve it.

It rang again, before he could silence it. Looking up from his phone, he saw a small lamp flying toward him. He dodged it and darted for the door.

"Sorry, they must have given me the wrong key," he said, in the deep and menacing modulated voice of Luke Taylor.

As he exited, he shouted back "carry on." He ran down the hallway, found the stairs, and rushed to escape being seen. Roland knew he would need to get back to his penthouse and dump the Taylor persona.

...

Zac couldn't catch the man before he left the room. He closed the door and fastened the additional security latch. He turned the lights on and hurried to the phone to call hotel security. And so on.

...

About seven years ago:

"Well, I'd like to thank you for being a participant," Heath said.

Vonnegut only nodded.

"I need to tell you something," Heath stated as he searched for the right words. He knew he needed to come clean. If he lied to Vonnegut about the ear completely, Vonnegut might find out soon. Vonnegut's General Practitioner was exceptional and the talk of Manhattan. Heath didn't need to tell him the whole truth but enough so Vonnegut would be careful.

Heath told Vonnegut that the experiment had impacted the production of fluid in Vonnegut's ear. He noted that it would probably go way in time, but

Vonnegut should be careful and try not to take stairs over the coming days.

"It may also affect your hearing," Heath added.

"Huh? Wha'dya say?" Vonnegut responded. He had heard every word, but it was fun to mess with people.

"It may impact your hearing," Heath repeated.

...

Roland ran down two flights of stairs. He stopped to catch his breath. Attempting to not look suspicious, he opened the door to the hallway, walked in, found the elevators, and headed back to the penthouse. Getting to the penthouse, he locked the door and rapidly worked to remove the Luke Taylor persona.

No one had followed him. He was safe. Roland knew he had to use the Paul Venter costume from now on. Venters would kill the traitor, Roland thought. But, where the hell was the traitor?

Roland looked at his phone to see who had called. A missed call from the private investigator lit up the screen. Roland wondered why the guy would be calling him this late. He called the private investigator back.

The private investigator answered.

"What's wrong?" the investigator questioned. He had had to step away from the blackjack table to get the call.

"You called me," Roland replied with frustration.

"No, I didn't," the private investigator responded.

"You sure as hell *did*," Roland said, getting bothered by this inconvenience.

"Hold on," the voice came back. Roland waited. The investigator checked his outgoing calls.

"Sorry, I must have butt-dialed you when I sat down at the blackjack table," he came back.

The investigator went on to tell Roland that he had new information but was going to call in the morning. Since he had Roland on the phone now, he would tell him it. As it was, the investigator informed Roland that the guy he was looking for had checked out of a Denver hotel the other day. In addition, the investigator had found that the guy had canceled his reservation at the upscale hotel in Vegas. The billionaire already knew this. A young couple was staying in that room and having passionate sex. The gambling addict went on to say he was trying to find out if the guy had checked into a different hotel in Vegas or had decided to drive straight through to Los Angeles.

"You have his hotel reservation in Los Angeles," Roland asked.

"Yeah, I called earlier today to confirm it," the gambler stated.

"Send me a text with it again," Roland said. Roland made up his mind that he would have to kill the traitor in the City of Angels.

"There's one more thing," the investigator said before hanging up, "there's a rumor that a judge is going to overturn your cease and desist."

Roland decided he would leave Vegas and spring a trap for the traitor in Los Angeles. He called to have the private plane ready itself for the trip. In the morning, he would call his lawyer to look into the rumor about the judge. To be safe, he would tell the private jet to be ready on a moments notice and have a flight plan to Bosnia drawn up. Roland's realtor had purchased a "vacation" home in Sarajevo at Roland's request. He could simply go to Bosnia on vacation, but he would stay if the pesky cops made more ground. Killing the traitor may be the last act on US soil, Roland thought.

The train tracks of the billionaire and those of the hetero-ally who loved equality were about to collide.

TWENTY-TWO

I woke from a deep sleep with dreams of Blossom still fresh in my mind. Checking out of the cheap and musty hotel, I hit the road and headed to the City of Angels. I was not in a hurry. My brother would not have time from work to see me until tomorrow, so when I got to Los Angeles, I would have almost a day to waste before getting to meet up with him.

...

To this point in the story, it has been made abundantly clear that Roland wanted to see the traitor dead. In his five-star hotel, he imagined the dead traitor. The image in his mind looked cartoonish. It looked like this:

Roland got dressed as Paul Venter. Upon flying late last night into Los Angeles, Roland had rented a car at the airport. He would need a way to get from his fancy hotel to the traitor's dive. Roland had decided to stay at another upscale hotel. It had five-star accommodations. From his incident with the young couple last night, he thought it best to be in a hotel separate from his intended victim. If he needed to escape, he would be able to drive further from the scene of the crime.

Driving his rental car, he encountered heavy traffic. He arrived at the rundown hotel after an hour and a half. No traffic and he would have been there in thirty minutes. Walking to the front counter, he gave the front desk worker the traitor's name and said he was a business associate.

"Has he checked in yet? We have a meeting soon," Venter stated with a slight giggle. His bushy, fake moustache had tickled him.

The desk staff told Venter that the person he sought had not only not arrived but had canceled his reservation.

He realized he should have simply called the sleazy hotel and asked rather than drive through traffic. Initially, he thought he would get the room number from them and bribe another maid for a master key.

Roland left infuriated and headed back to his fancy hotel. He hit rush-hour traffic and was boiling over with anger. The load of troubles coupled with the traffic overloaded what little rationality he had. When a car would not let him merge to the right so that he could exit, he drew his revolver and waved it at them. They let him in but flipped him off as he exited.

...

Compared to the 11-hour excursion I had done the previous day, the trip from Sin City to the City of Angels was a breeze. I was there in no time. Parking, I went into the five-star hotel and checked in. Its accommodations would be a needed contrast to the musty and stinky dwelling which housed me last night.

284

I got all my stuff out of the trunk of my car and took it to my room. It was getting close to dinner time, and I contemplated what I should have. On the nightstand was a flyer for a pizza joint. It didn't deliver, but the text on the bottom announced that it would give a free small pizza to any hotel guest who showed their reservation. That was it. I would have pizza.

I went to the three elevators on my floor and pressed the down button. The front desk would know how to get to the pizzeria. I would ask them. If it was close, I would walk. If it was far, I'd drive.

...

Roland pulled into the parking garage of the upscale hotel. He parked his car next to one with Massachusetts plates. Being so focused on his task, he didn't notice it. He needed to call the investigator and find out where the hell the traitor was.

Roland walked to the front desk to ask where the nearest five-star restaurant was. The desk was staffed by a single person. The young lady was gabbing on the phone with her boyfriend. She ignored Roland.

Feeling there was no time to waste, he reached over the counter and clicked to hang up the phone. The young lady was pissed but didn't lose her cool. The last time she had lost her composure, she had been written up. She didn't want to be written up again.

"Where's the nearest fine restaurant?" Roland asked with a fake smile that matched his moustache.

The desk worker handed him a brochure that listed the various restaurants in the area and ranked them from five-star to no-stars. Roland thanked her in a condescending manner. He headed to the elevators and pressed the up button.

···

My stomach growled as I entered the elevator on my left. I went down.

···

Roland entered the middle elevator and went up.

···

As I approached the front desk, I heard the voice of the sole attendant explaining to someone that she didn't hang up on him. Some asshole did, she claimed. She was apologizing profusely, and from the sound of things, she was talking to her significant other.

She was so engaged in her conversation that I didn't want to interrupt. But, I needed to know where the pizzeria was. I held up the flyer that I had brought from my nightstand and mouthed the word "where?" She held up one finger to inform me to wait a minute.

"Yeah, uh huh, yeah," she mumbled into the phone as she wrote the directions down for the pizza joint. It looked to be within walking distance. I was in the good part of town. What could possibly happen to me? I thought. I headed out of the hotel to go get my free pizza.

···

Listen:

Roland called the private investigator to find if he had any clue where the traitor was. The investigator said that his contacts in Los Angeles were scouring the area for the person, and he would call the moment any information came in.

Roland changed out of his Paul Venter persona. There was no reason for a disguise. He didn't know where the traitor was. He headed to the parking garage on his way to have some fine cuisine.

· · ·

But to continue:

I arrived at the pizza joint with my appetite high. Showing my hotel reservation to the cashier, he informed me that the deal ended two weeks ago. Oh well, I thought, I'm already here, I should just eat. Ordering a slice of pepperoni and a drink, I sat and waited for my order to arrive. In no time, the order was done. I bit into the repulsive slice. It tasted like tree bark covered with spaghetti sauce and curdled milk. Hungry, I ate it anyway. I now knew why they were giving it out for free.

· · ·

On the way to his rental car, Roland spotted a silver, luxury car parked next to his rental. It was a nice shade of silver that would look wonderful on one of his corvettes, he thought. Wait, he had seen this car before, he reflected. Roland hurried over to the back of the car. Massachusetts plates slapped him in the face. What were the chances that a car with Massachusetts plates would be in Vegas yesterday at the hotel the traitor was suppose to be at and now, here, in the city that the traitor was planning to come? Roland knew it was no coincident. The Creator of the Universe was sending Roland a message. The traitor was staying in the five-star hotel. It was time for him to die. Roland didn't want to let down the Creator of the Universe.

Roland ran back to the hotel's front desk. Since he had lost his disguise, he had to be careful how he acted or what he said. He held up an image of the individual he had been endlessly tracking.

"Do you know what room this guy is in?" he said to the girl who was still on the phone with her boyfriend.

"Hold on," she stated to the other on the phone.

"Yeah, but I can't release room numbers," she asserted authoritatively.

Roland told her that the guy had won a lot of money but had a short time to claim his prize. To show that he was being authentic, he flashed a thousand dollars in front of her. It was all a lie. Like you, I hate being lied to.

"Well," she paused, "if it's for a good reason, I guess I can tell you, but he isn't in his room. He left a little while back to have pizza."

Roland informed her that she had done the right thing. The guy would get a great surprise soon, Roland told her with a huge smile.

Pausing to form a strategy, Roland wondered whether he should go to the maid and get a master key or head to the pizzeria. If he got the key, he would have to wait until the traitor returned to the hotel room. He had waited long enough for this moment. Roland decided it would be best to rush to the pizza joint and kidnap the traitor at gun point when the traitor left. Having a vehicle, Roland could take him to some desolate place and end his miserable existence.

Roland ran to the car, put the pizzeria's address in his GPS, and headed to finish his journey. He was shaking with excitement.

...

As I ate the horrid pizza, it happened again. A thought bubble violated the privacy of my psyche. Pulling a pen from my pocket, I wrote two sentences on a napkin, and the event passed. The two sentences read:

I once graded my work Breakfast of Champions a "C." This work will make amends for that by using all the images I doodled for Breakfast in a new way.

Putting the napkin in my front pocket with my pen, I left the pizzeria and headed back to the 5-star hotel. The sun had set, and twilight had arrived.

...

As it was:

Roland was driving down the street to the pizzeria. He saw the traitor walking on the sidewalk going the opposite direction. At the next stoplight, Roland got in the left turn lane and made a U-turn. He was overwhelmed with excitement.

...

As I walked back to the hotel, I thought of my brother. How nice it would be to see him tomorrow, I reflected. Someone said something to my left. I took another step, then realized they were talking to me.

"Take another step, and I will shoot you where you stand," the voice said.

I froze. Nervously, I turned to my left slowly. There, on the side of the street, a car had pulled next to the curb and had its passenger window down. The driver was pointing a gun at me.

"Get in the car, now," the person demanded. I didn't know what to do. I felt stuck in time. The amber of the moment needed to thaw for me to act. I took a step toward the car. What the hell am I doing? I thought, I'm just giving him a closer target if he shoots. My brain raced to find an answer to my dilemma. My pause must have alerted the gun-wielding criminal that I was plotting.

"Get in the fucking car, *now*," he shouted.

I scanned up and down the street. There was no one to yell to for help. A half a block up on the right I did, however, notice a narrow alley. If I could make it there, I might have a chance. Formulating a plan, I realized if I darted now, the crazy man may shoot me where I stood.

My heart was racing, but in an ultra-calm voice, I said, "Hold up, I need to tie my shoe." I bent down and acted as if my right shoe was untied. The act had bought me a little time.

...

Roland was so blinded by the drive to kill the traitor that he was not thinking clearly. He tried to kidnap the guy at gunpoint without getting out of the car. For a moment, Roland thought he saw fear in the traitor's eyes, but the fear had seemed to quickly dissipate. That arrogant prick was tying his shoe at gunpoint.

...

290

I really did tie my shoes. Both of them. I was about to run, and I didn't want either shoe to trip me up and lead to my demise.

As I started to stand up, I didn't stand straight up. Instead, I shifted my weight and stood up and to the right. I used my upward momentum to dash toward the alley. My heart was racing. He was going to shoot at any moment, I thought. I should have considered weaving or zig zagging to be a harder target to hit, but my sole focus was getting to that alley. So, I made a beeline straight for it.

...

Things were not going as Roland had planned them. He aimed the revolver and readied it to fire. The headlights from a car coming from behind ricocheted off his rearview mirror and blinded him. When he could see again, the traitor was gone.

...

I made it to the alley and didn't slow down. Climbing a fence, I rushed across an empty lot. To my left was a ditch and train tracks. The tracks would lead me back to the hotel where I could call for help. Sprinting, I crossed the ditch and darted down the tracks.

A few weeks back, an old woman had sprinted to a bus to avoid me. She would have won bronze in the '72 Olympics. Now, I ran with more fear than she had. I would have had gold.

...

Roland was angry with himself for having not captured the traitor. That prick could now identify me, he thought, I have to kill him before he notifies authorities. The traitor would likely run back to familiar territory, the hotel. Roland hit the gas and hurried to get to the hotel.

...

Racing into the lobby of the hotel, I saw the young girl still on the phone with her boyfriend. I didn't stop. Had I been thinking, I would have had her call the police immediately. I wasn't thinking. I was reacting. My room had a phone, and I would lock the door and call them. I would be safe soon. Blinded by my adrenaline, I didn't want to wait for the elevator. Taking the stairs two and three at a time, I arrived on my floor in no time.

...

Parking his car in the garage, Roland exited it as if it were on fire. He was running. There was too much at risk, now. Twenty meters from the car, he stopped. He had left the handgun on the passenger's seat. He hurried back to retrieve it.

...

I closed the door and locked it. Had I been thinking, I would have also used the security latch. I wasn't thinking. I was trying to survive.

I rushed to the room's phone. Grabbing the receiver, I dialed 911. There was no dial tone. There was no ringing. What the hell? I thought. Looking down, I realized that in my excitement I had ripped the cord from the phone. I frantically tried to put it back into its socket. It was broke.

Remembering my cellphone, I went quickly to the duffle bag to retrieve it. It was dead. So it goes.

...

Wondering what to do, I started to leave the room. Maybe the solution to my problem was somewhere else. Opening the door, I scanned the hall. Near the end of the hall, a man had his back to me. He had a gun holstered in the small of his back. It was too dangerous to leave, I thought. Not thinking, I grabbed the Please Do Not Disturb sign and hung it on my door. I knew it wouldn't provide any protection, but I did it anyway. The sign looked like this:

I closed the door quietly and contemplated my next move.

•••

The thing was:

The man at the end of the hall was an off-duty police officer. He was meeting his mistress in one of the rooms, but he had already earned a number of awards for his heroics in the line of duty. Had I called out to him, he could have been my salvation. It was hard to tell good guys from bad guys when guns were involved.

•••

I decided hiding may be my best option. Scanning the room, there were few choices. I got in the closet and tried to be quiet. A hotel guest in an adjacent room was playing the second movement of Beethoven's 7th symphony. It brought an eerie presence to the moment.

•••

Roland found the maid. She was a portly Hispanic woman with bad teeth. Her English was good enough that a transaction could take place. He would give her $1492, and she would give him the master key. It was all the cash that Roland had on him. He headed to the elevator to go to the traitor's room.

•••

In the closet, I started to wonder why I was hiding. Did the guy even know where I was staying? The guy looked like the famous billionaire, Kevin

Roland, but why would he want to kill me? If it was him, he would surely have the resources to track me down. I stayed put.

Then, it hit me. Another thought bubble.

I had no choice. I had to get out of the closet and type. The laptop was already up and running. My fingers flew as I typed the thought. It read:

> *I got into the closet. I was no coward, but I didn't want to fight. Hopefully, Roland would not find me. Roland entered the room with his gun drawn. He would kill that vile and disgusting creature. Then, he would be off to Bosnia. He would become A Man Without a Country. Roland didn't care. He searched the place, but it appeared that the cockroach was not there. Then, he noticed the computer on. He read the text. Well, the first two sentences, at least. Roland knew the traitor was in the closet. He went to the closet, opened the door, and found the traitor begging for his life. A blissful rush came over Roland as he fired a single round into the forehead of the traitor. The traitor was dead. So it goes.*

...

The thing was:

The story on the screen that glared back at me was from Vonnegut's thoughts in the TT machine. It should have an asterisk after it. An asterisk looked like this:

It is not, however, what happened.

•••

I read over the words I had just written. As I started to cry, I realized there was only one thing left for me to do.

•••

Roland got to the traitor's door. A "Do Not Disturb" sign hung from it. Placing the master key in the electronic slot, Roland entered the hotel room. Closing the door, he withdrew the revolver with its silencer already attached. He walked slowly into the dim-lit space.

•••

I heard the door open and close. Roland was here. Sweat beaded on my brow, and I tried to control my breathing. My heart was racing.

...

Roland scanned the room and saw no sign of the traitor. Where was he? Roland thought. Then, Roland noticed the laptop was on and text was on its screen. He walked over and read it. A devious smile came to his face. He walked through the bedroom door of the suite and headed to the closet.

Unlike the destiny expounded on the page of text, Roland did not wait to open the closet. He fired three rounds into it. Thump, thump, thump came as the bullets pierced the wooden door.

Roland walked over to the door and opened it. It was empty. Confused, he scratched his head. Then, he heard a noise behind him.

...

I, too, asserted my free will. There were no train tracks here. Coming from behind the bedroom door, I pointed my grandpa's double-barrel, loaded with my father's buckshot, at the man who had shot a closet door.

...

Roland spun around in time to see the wrong end of a double-barrel shotgun. It looked like this:

He started to raise his arm to fire the revolver at the traitor. I pulled both triggers and unloaded buckshot into his face. Kevin Dwayne Roland, and all his various personas, expired along with this story. So it goes.

EPILOGUE

Listen:

As a celebrity, Vonnegut was given personalized transportation back to his home in Manhattan. The other participants of the TT experiment were stacked in vans and busses, but Vonnegut was taken in a private sedan to the isolated airport to be flown directly back to New York.

Like their trip to the facility, everyone had to have a bag over their head. Vonnegut was no exception. Unlike the others, however, Vonnegut's bag was removed as soon as he landed in New York.

The TT agents took him to his Manhattan home and thanked him for his participation.

"It was nothing," Vonnegut responded. It had given him a chance to write this final novel, and he saw nothing harmful to the time he devoted to the enterprise.

Opening his front door, Vonnegut was exhausted. He walked up the staircase of his home to get to his familiar bed and get some shut eye. The comfort of his bed would feel like a hug from a loved one. It was familiar and needed.

His ears still ached and his head was spinning. Vonnegut stumbled and landed on the bed. It was as if his mind and legs were not in unison. For Vonnegut, balance occurred at the cost of tremendous focus and attention. What the hell have they done to me? Vonnegut thought.

Vonnegut wanted to get off of his unreliable legs. Pulling down the comforter, he lay down and closed his eyes. He *fell* asleep in no time.

...

His dreams were filled with homicidal beavers, suicidal French women, masquerading criminals, social rallies, cosmic coincidences, genetically-altered cows, scatological humor, and sci-fi fantasy. Train tracks and free will fought an epic battle in the temporally non-linear narrative. Just like existence itself, the dream was complicated and absurd. He slept, but he smiled.

...

Mid-April, seven years ago:
Vonnegut woke. He thought he should get up and get some coffee. There was much he needed to complete today.

The university in Ilium had invited Vonnegut to speak to inspiring college writers. Vonnegut always looked forward to shaping young, energetic writers. But, Vonnegut hadn't worked on his presentation much. His speech was a few scraps of notes piled on the desk in his den.

He went to the desk to begin to pull the disparate elements together. Rummaging through the pile of fragments, he couldn't think of the theme he wanted them to have. Coffee would help, he thought. He stood up and went to get some java. His legs betrayed him. Almost falling, he steadied himself using the back of the desk chair. He let out a sigh.

The kitchen was downstairs. Vonnegut made his way to the staircase. He headed down. So it goes.

R I P

****

KURT VONNEGUT
1922-2007

A GREAT AMERICAN
WRITER

(REGARDLESS OF
WHAT FOXNEWS
SAYS)

RIP, stood for Rest in Peace, I had to laugh. Even the dead liked acronyms.

Made in the USA
Charleston, SC
14 August 2014